About the author

Paula Jane Rodgers is a professionally trained secretary with nearly thirty years' experience. She has spent the last few years writing *Enlightenment*, a horror story, which is the sequel to *Curator Angelus*. She is currently working on the last book in the trilogy.

ENLIGHTENMENT

Paula Jane Rodgers

ENLIGHTENMENT

Vanguard Press

VANGUARD PAPERBACK

© Copyright 2020
Paula Jane Rodgers

A CIP catalogue record for this title is
available from the British Library.

ISBN 978 1 784658 18 2

*Vanguard Press is an imprint of
Pegasus Elliot MacKenzie Publishers Ltd.*
www.pegasuspublishers.com

First Published in 2020

**Vanguard Press
Sheraton House Castle Park
Cambridge England**

Printed & Bound in Great Britain

Dedication

To my husband, Richard, who continues to
encourage and support me.

Chapter One
The Encounter

Kicking off her slippers, Lisa Brook tucked up her feet and rested her head against one of the plumped-up cushions on the arm of the sofa. She aimed the remote control at the television and pressed the 'on' button, but as she flicked through the stations, she found that there wasn't anything that she wanted to watch.

Lisa had taken the day off work and her mother had taken her son out for a treat that day. Elizabeth Caplin and Peter Oates were going to a wildlife park and afterwards they were going onto a restaurant to overindulge in pizza and ice-cream. Excited, he had got up earlier than usual that morning as he loved his trips out with his grandmother.

It was rare that Lisa got any alone time and she was going to make the most of it. After her nap, she would dye her hair and paint her nails. But first, she would allow herself to rest. Her eyes soon tired and she drifted off into a deep sleep. It was there that she encountered one of her out-of-body experiences. They were becoming more frequent and the overhead vision of herself no longer took her by surprise. She gazed down and noted how peaceful she looked. It was usual for her not to leave the confines of the room where she slept, but on this occasion, she left her body behind and travelled much further.

It took little time for Lisa to make the journey from her home in the Lake District as she flew through the air over numerous hills, roads, houses and waterways. No solid structure proved to be an obstacle as she passed through each one with ease. Her destination was Beechwood village.

Lisa watched the goings-on at Fred Hurst's retirement party from the furthest nook of the ceiling in his junk shop. They had never been in each other's lives, but she appeared to be there to observe her grandfather and his guests' behaviour. She was there for a reason, for which she would later discover.

Neither Fred nor anyone else in the shop was able to see Lisa. It wasn't because they couldn't, but on account that no one had taken the time to notice. Nobody ever seems to bother to look up into the corners of a room.

During the course of the morning, the sky had already seen several shades of grey. A lingering chill had made its presence known and caused it to feel a good deal fresher than the day before. Crisp leaves blew around on the ground, no two were ever the same shade. Several of them swirled in a circular motion, as though playing chase, outside the window of Fred's shop. The smell of wood blazing in log burners filled the air and drifted inside when the door was opened. Fred thought that it was possible that winter would put in an early appearance, which signified that yet another lonely year had gone by.

Celebrations were well under way as a number of Fred's acquaintances congregated in the front of his shop. The wooden floorboards creaked beneath their feet. His guests were, in the main, loyal customers and folks that worked in other establishments in Beechwood. Bringing along balloons and banners, a couple of them had taken the time to decorate the front window, door and the long wooden sales counter that ran the length of the shop. A selection of nibbles, which were supplied by a local catering company, remained untouched. Sounds of frivolity drifted out and along the road as his guests chatted and laughed, getting louder as the hours went by. A steady flow of well-wishers had called in during the morning to present him with birthday and retirement gifts, which were received with thanks.

Linda Hays, a psychic and volunteer at the community charity shop was standing in the doorway with her habitual cigarette propped between the nicotine stained index and middle fingers of her left hand. She looked older than her years with skin that was thickened and discoloured with a tinge of yellow. And, she had a phlegmy cough to boot. Her undernourished body was the result of skipped meals which were often replaced with a cigarette or two. Fred watched her with interest as she blew smoke rings, of varying sizes, in between

11

taking sips of white wine from her glass. Her little finger pointed upwards. Sporadic wafts of cool air drifted in through the opening of the door, but it also drew in her cigarette smoke. *Should I ask her to move away from the door? Is she even aware of what she's doing to herself, never mind anyone else?* Fred decided not to say anything; after all, she was a guest that had taken time out to wish him well.

Derek Mole and his wife, Sylvia, would often call into Fred's shop if they were passing and look for anything that they might be able to upcycle. Derek was pouring Sylvia yet another glass of white wine. Her drinks were going down fast and he looked at her with an anxious expression. He wanted her to slow down; however, he did not say anything, but he never dared to. The couple had moved into the Parkins old family home a few years earlier and were close to finishing their renovations. The refurbishment had met with two significant incidents. There was a plumber who had somehow managed to fall through the bathroom floor. He suffered two broken legs. And there was a plasterer who slipped down a full flight of stairs. He fractured his skull. Both of them gave similar reports of seeing apparitions and hearing strange sounds before each of their accidents happened.

For months, Fred had counted down to this special birthday and had crossed each day off his wall calendar, every morning, with a thick black marker pen. His retirement, at last, had arrived. He'd had a couple of drinks and yet he felt deflated and not in the mood for celebrating. He was not even in the right frame of mind for any of his guests' small talk. Had the realisation of this day, after so many years of waiting, become all too real? Perhaps it was because of sleep deprivation—his apprehension being the main reason for him tossing and turning through the previous nights.

Needing to escape, Fred went to stand behind the counter. He put on his new reading glasses and opened up the local newspaper—*The Beechwood Chronicle*. The days had long since gone where he would turn straight to the back pages to look at the sporting section. He had developed an unhealthy habit of reading through the obituaries first and looking down each of the columns for familiar names. He recognised one name, a Mr Timothy Parker, but when he looked at the birth date, he realised that it had to be a different one, as the birth year was later. *Perhaps he's a son or relative.*

Fred stopped reading when he caught sight of a sudden movement out of the corner of his eye. There was someone or something in the storeroom that was at the back of the shop. He looked over at the opened storeroom door before he checked on his guests. It wasn't any of them that were in there, as they were all accounted for. They were still partying and seemed unaware of what he had seen; however, he noticed that their laughter and chatting appeared muffled as though they were distant or underwater. He turned to look towards the storeroom again.

In the past, Fred had witnessed strange happenings inside his shop, but had chosen to ignore them. On this occasion, however, it was different and impossible to overlook as the sighting was accompanied by the sound of deep breathing. There was an unpleasant, yet familiar smell which appeared to fill the room. It was that unmistakable smell of death and it always had an accompanying taste that hit the back of your throat, which would, in turn, force its way up into your sinuses and down deep within your lungs. It was natural for him to start coughing as he struggled to relieve the tightness that he felt inside his chest. The feeling subsided and he managed to catch his breath, before he noticed that a black shadow was being followed by a number of what looked like smaller versions of it. *What the hell was that? I hope they're just passing through or is there a particular reason as to why they're lurking in my storeroom? Is it the Angel of Death himself that's come for me? I hope not! I didn't notice if it was carrying a scythe.*

Feeling drawn to whatever awaited him, Fred felt compelled to investigate and although he was aware that he may have imagined it all, he gave it no further thought as he made his way towards the storeroom. He walked at a slow pace as the spring in his step had long since gone. Upon him reaching the doorway, the heavy breathing ceased. He wiped his clammy palms down the front of his trousers and turned around to slide the rolling ladder along, so that he was able to reach an aerosol can from one of the uppermost shelves. Shaking it close to his ear, he estimated that it was half full. The plastic lid had bonded with the rusty rim of the can, however. He managed to loosen it, albeit splitting the lid on one side. Pulling the lid off, it flew out of his hand and landed a few feet away on the floor. Testing the aerosol, he pressed his index finger down on the nozzle. It released a quick spray of lavender. He was armed in case he needed to defend himself against any potential intruder. He could spray it in their eyes.

Leaning against the door frame, Fred looked around the storeroom before he dared to step inside, but his vision was blurred, and his surroundings were out of focus. After realising his predicament, he reached up and pulled his reading glasses further down the bridge of his nose. The room appeared empty of any signs of life. He walked around the room as though whoever or whatever it was had managed to find a hiding place. There was no evidence to suggest that anyone had entered or made any attempts to, but he could feel that someone was watching him.

Moving unnoticed from the front of the shop to a corner of the storeroom ceiling, Lisa continued to observe. She flinched when she got close to a spider's web that was hung like fine lace and smiled when she remembered that it could not touch her. Glancing around the room, she noticed that it was almost empty. There was bare wooden shelving leaning against two of the walls. The only sound in the room was from a dripping tap as the droplets of water bounced inside the old metal sink.

Fred had stopped noticing the horrible stench. He was not sure if it had gone or if he had got used to it. The bell above the shop door rang out. He remembered that he had guests and turned around to walk back into the front of the shop. Except, he wasn't able to. He was forced to watch on and felt helpless, when he found that he was frozen to the spot and unable to make any attempt to stop the storeroom door as it began to creak and close in front of him. It clicked shut.

Trapped inside the storeroom, Fred noticed that the smell was present and did appear to be getting stronger. It turned his stomach and made him feel nauseous. He gagged and cupped the palm of his left hand over his nose and mouth. Able to move again, he threw the can onto the floor and reached forward to open the door with his right hand. He grabbed hold of the handle and tried to pull it down, but he was forced to let go as it started to glow red like a burning ember.

Yanking his hand back, Fred spread out his fingers to examine the damage. A number of adjoining open blisters had presented themselves over his palm and along every soft pad of his fingers and thumb. The pain intensified as the flesh beneath his sores bubbled with the retained heat. He needed to get to the first aid box, and fast, but he couldn't as it was located to the front of the shop, underneath the counter, along with the keys to the back door of the storeroom. On second thoughts, he would need to get himself to the Accident and Emergency Department at the local hospital, but he had left his mobile telephone on one of the shelves to the front.

Moving his hand away from his nose and mouth, Fred pounded the side of his fist on the door. The wood seemed to soften, and his thumping sounded distant. "Help," he shouted. "Can any of you hear me? I can't get out. This flaming door's stuck." He stared at the smouldering handle, willing it to stop burning and for someone on the other side to move it. He waited a moment longer before he banged on the door again. *Why is nobody coming? Can't they hear me?* He put his ear to the door and listened, but he was met with an eerie silence. *That's strange. Have they all left without bothering to say goodbye?* He tried to remain calm, despite his realisation that he had become trapped inside his storeroom without any way of communicating with the outside world. He concentrated on his breathing and tried not to hyperventilate. This was not a normal situation and he would need to keep his wits about him.

The dripping tap caught Fred's attention. Its cold water was enticing. At least it would take the edge off his pain and relieve some of his suffering. His body temperature had risen as sweat beads rolled down his brow and over his nose. Yet, vapour from his breath was visible as the room's temperature plummeted. He let out an audible groan as he attempted to walk across the room towards the sink. It felt like a longer distance than it should have done.

Time appeared to standstill as the room around him started to spin.

A fingertip or a talon began stroking Fred. He could not be certain which, but whichever it was, it did not scratch him. It made him shudder, though, as it started at the top of his back and worked its way down his spine. Ignoring it, he stood in front of the sink and propped himself against it until his dizziness had passed.

Fred was right-handed and using his left hand was proving an awkward task as the tap felt stiff and harder to turn than usual. The level of pain in his right hand had reached intolerable and he needed to cool it down, and fast. Straining his left wrist, he tried to use more force. His wrist joint clicked as he managed to loosen the tap. The flow of water jolted into action after some initial hammering and spluttering. He allowed its flow to hit the underside of his wrist and it continued to run down over his pulsating palm and fingers.

Fred's energy levels weakened as the entity moved up right behind him. It grew stronger and denser as it stretched up vertically, absorbing any available energy from its surroundings. Fred's hand would prove to be the least of his worries as he felt his chest tighten again. With no alternative, he knew that sooner or later he would have to face whatever it was that was desperate for his attention and that resistance was not a given option. He turned his head.

Unsure what would greet him, Fred looked upwards, but there was nothing to focus on. It was a black mass with no apparent features. His memory was not what it used to be, but he could recollect those nights that he had spent with his son, Peter Hurst, in Beechwood Park. *Is it possible that all this, that is happening right now, is somehow connected to that?* With his hand placed beneath the running water, he continued to look behind him as he tried to work out what was happening. "Who are you?" he asked with a slight tremor present in his tone. "More to the point, what are you and what do you want with me?"

The entity did not respond and made no attempts to communicate.

It was not until Fred was about to look away that the distorted outlines of a stranger's face started to emerge on the entity. The features changed after several seconds to a face that he was not familiar with. Each time, a transformation presented an expression of blankness. Fred's eyes widened after a realisation that the entity was there to collect his soul and all the faces that he saw were other souls that were trapped inside it. The entity moved up close until both of them almost occupied the same space.

The tap continued to gush, but Fred seemed unaware that his hand was no longer beneath the flow of water. The slide show of faces stopped and returned to a blackness. Fred turned away and placed his hand back beneath the water. For a moment, he contemplated running. *But where would that get me? I'm an old man and there's nowhere for me to go. I've got no choice; I'll just have to wait and see what fate as in store for me.*

Fred did not have to wait long until the entity made its next move. It extended out its defined, yet featherless, wings. Their span was wide, and the tips touched the walls on the two opposing sides of the room. Each wing was longer than the entity was tall. It folded one of its wings inwards and wrapped it around Fred's body. He did not struggle as the entity moved its other wing in an up-and-down motion and started to ascend. *Where the hell is it taking me?*

Lisa watched on. *What can I do to help him? I'm not even sure I know what that thing is.* The storeroom door swung open and slammed against the wall, beneath her. A rush of cool air filled the room. Fred was not able to turn around to see who it was. He wanted to shout out to them, to tell them to leave, to get out and run for their lives, but he was struggling to breathe, let alone yell.

A black shadow entered and commanded, "Let him go. Put my father down. You are taking him nowhere. Do you hear me?"

The entity did not move. It had Fred in its grasp as it hovered inches above the floor.

Fred felt an uncontrollable urge to be with Peter. *I need to protect my boy.* He started to wriggle in an attempt to get away from the entity. *But, how's that even possible when I can't even defend myself?*

20

The entity loosened its grip and twisted its head to look at who dared to confront it. Of course, it knew the black shadow and its place in the pecking order, but it dared to defy it and tightened its hold as it challenged the powers of the black shadow in a predictable battle of the demons.

The black shadow held back. It had nothing to prove.

The entity turned to look at the black shadow. It wanted to know why the other remained silent. It looked up and noticed Lisa.

The bell above the shop door rang out.

The black shadow, the entity and Lisa were gone.

Fred gasped for breath. His legs had weakened and gave way beneath him. As he sat on the floor, he looked around the room and noted that he was alone. The handle on the storeroom door had returned to normal. He examined his hand; the pain was gone, and his sores had healed.

He felt a welcoming breeze blowing through from the opened shop door. Reaching up to the sink with his left hand, Fred tried to pull himself up, but to no avail as what little energy he had left was not enough. Resting, he remained on the floor. He looked over towards the door and hoped that someone would shout or walk through to see where he was, but no one did. *Why did the bell sound out if there doesn't appear to be anyone there? And where has my son gone?*

It felt like an age before Fred attempted to stand again. He manoeuvred his body so that his legs were out in front of him. Mustering all his strength, he bent both of his knees, put his hands down onto the floor to either side of him and managed to push himself up. Brushing himself down, he was ready for his retirement to begin.

Chapter Two
Robert Caplin

Robert Caplin was a sociable gentleman who dressed in smart attire. He was an affluent member of the local community, who at first appearance, seemed to be very much respected. He owned a large house which was set back from the water. He was the proprietor of The Red Squirrel public house and owner of a magnificent hotel which overlooked one of the most visited lakes in the district.

Elizabeth had moved out of Lisa's apartment and in with Robert a little while after meeting him in The Red Squirrel. He had told her that she was to make herself at home and that was what she did. Every day she made it known to Eliza, their maid, and Harry, their gardener, what jobs she needed them to do when they had finished with their usual chores. She was hesitant at first as she had expected to feel awkward about giving out any instructions, but she felt quite comfortable about it because they were both such approachable and willing employees.

Eliza had already worked with Robert for several months. She was young with a small amount of experience; though, she was eager to learn and appeared to be able to take in anything new that she was shown. She was lasting longer than any of her predecessors as they had found it difficult when coping with the man of the house.

Harry, on the other hand, was a long-serving employee. He was an elderly gentleman who refused to retire. He believed that once you gave up working then you might as well admit that you were ready to give up on life. He was a slow worker, but he got the job done and had a keen eye for detail. He had aches and pains, like anyone of a similar age, but what else was there to do? He found daytime television tedious and he lived in a small flat without a balcony. He had no family and always said that he was getting paid for doing the work that he loved. It was a win-win situation for him. It was not the best paid job in the world, but there was always someone worse off. He and Robert were not the best of friends, but they were used to each other's quirky ways and got on just fine.

From the first time that Robert had set eyes on Elizabeth, he knew that she was the woman for him. Of course, he had noticed the unflattering glasses perched on her nose but had looked beyond them. Over the years he had met his fair share of superficial women. Trollops that had smelt his money from a hundred metres. Those types were easy to come across; however, he realised that Elizabeth was genuine. He could tell that she was caring from the way that she acted towards those around her. He soon became fond of her and saw something in her beyond the dowdy exterior. At first, he did not realise that she did not know any better and that she felt comfortable that way. He wanted her to see what he could see. She needed to come out of her shell and blossom into the beautiful individual that he knew she was already.

Robert had asked his work associate's girlfriends and wives to get in touch with their hairdressers, nail technicians and beauticians. One of each arrived at his home the next morning to take care of Elizabeth. A chauffeur-driven white limousine pulled up onto their drive that same afternoon with a personal shopper to escort her around the local boutiques. On that first shopping trip, she sneaked a peek at the price tags and was not able to comprehend how expensive some of the items were. She compared the cost to what else she could buy for that type of money. Her walk-in wardrobe was brimming with new clothes, shoes and accessories. At first, she had found it difficult because she was not used to a lavish lifestyle or the person in the mirror that looked back at her, but she knew that she could make herself adjust.

Roberts's proposal had taken Elizabeth by surprise. It was after they had dined out with a client and his wife. She had felt out of her depth as they ate in an up-market restaurant. For most of the evening she was not sure what the conversation had been about and would smile and laugh when the others did. She felt foolish when she had to copy Robert because she did not know how she should be eating her lobster thermidor. She tried not to look obvious, but she was sure that they had all noticed.

Robert was grinning all the way home in the back of the taxi. He held Elizabeth's hand as he stared through the windscreen and never spoke a word. She presumed that his silly face was because he was intoxicated, and she had no idea what he had planned.

Robert and Elizabeth arrived home. He led her to one of the sofas and gestured for her to sit. He turned around and half tripped over the corner of the rug. Hurrying up the stairs, he somehow managed not to miss a step. He returned with a small blue velvet box grasped inside his hand and got down on one knee. It was like a scene from one of them romance novels that she liked to read. He coughed to clear his throat, looked up at her and said, "Will you marry me?" His words were slurred, but despite him being drunk, he had managed to put them in the right order.

The ring took her breath away. It was an eighteen-carat white gold band with a three-carat round diamond.

"Yes," Elizabeth replied without hesitating. *I wonder if this is the same ring that belonged to his late wife,* she had thought as she visualised Robert pulling it off Diane's finger as she lay in her open coffin.

Robert slipped the ring onto the correct finger. The fit was perfect. He struggled to get to his feet. Elizabeth rose from the sofa and put her hands in his to help him up. The two of them fell onto the sofa before they embraced and laughed.

Robert left nothing to chance and the next day he had set the wedding date. He did not want to give Elizabeth the chance to change her mind.

The service took place several weeks later inside his hotel. Robert's staff took care of the arrangements. The reception and evening party followed within the grounds of their home. There was a marquee in the garden with tables that were adorned with lengths of white lace and there were arrangements of white flowers which included roses, tulips, carnations and daffodils. A number of young men and ladies were dressed in black-and-white outfits as they waited on the guests and served flutes of champagne. It was a private and lavish occasion with a few relatives that could make the trip from Elizabeth's side and Robert invited countless business colleagues. No invitations had been sent out to any of his family and he did not have any children that he was aware of. His family wanted nothing to do with him. They had disowned him years ago. He was the black sheep of the family and for reasons he had not explained.

Elizabeth had not needed to fret about anything apart from choosing her dress. She could pick any one that she wanted and did not need to concern herself with the cost. With no worries, all she had to do was relax and let the hairdresser and beautician work their magic.

There were two photographers on hand that day. One of them took the posed pictures whilst the other took pictures of the spontaneous moments.

The dress was stunning. Lisa had gasped when she saw Elizabeth showing it off as she entered the dining area on the day of the wedding. It looked expensive and must have taken someone hours to make, by hand. Her hair was fastened up and she wore a subtle tiara. Natural shades of make-up were applied to emphasise her features and the contact lenses she had worn made her look unrecognisable. The scarred tissue across her chest had lost its harsh redness as she stood proud in her sequinned white dress. It tapered in at the waist and its hemline dropped to just below her knees. Her shoes were coordinated with an innocence of white that matched the bouquet that she clasped with both hands. Her nails revealed a recent manicure and were painted a subtle pink. She looked happy, younger and her eyes twinkled as she laughed when Peter questioned, "Who's that lady, Mummy?"

Lisa had bought herself a blue dress for the wedding and she could wear it during the summer months. She already owned a pair of shoes and a bag that would match. Peter wore a grey suit, white shirt and grey bow tie. It was one of those with the elastic that is hidden underneath the collar. His new shoes were kept in the box until the ceremony. She had wanted to keep his entire outfit away from him until the ceremony, but he was insistent that he wore them and so the two of them decided on a compromise before they got into the car.

Lisa had set the alarm early that morning and had driven there in the same car that she had owned for a number of years. It was reliable and she wanted to keep it for a while longer. Robert wanted to upgrade it to something bigger, but she did not want to drive around in an expensive car that she would not be able to afford to run. She was glad that Elizabeth was happy and had found someone to take care of her; however, his controlling ways were of concern to her and how had he managed to gain such wealth?

Robert had told Elizabeth that his late wife was a wealthy woman and he inherited his fortune from her; however, what Elizabeth didn't know was that while that was the truth, he had failed to mention that he had drug runners working for him around the clock and that one of his favourite pastimes was the buying and selling of counterfeit and stolen goods.

Peter had managed, for the most part, to remain still throughout the ceremony with a small amount of fidgeting. Every time he moved; he would turn to look at Lisa to see if she had noticed. Of course she had, but she had never expected him to sit perfectly still, so she said nothing. The fact that she had bribed him beforehand was the major factor for his good behaviour. On the morning of the wedding it was verbally agreed between the two of them, that if he acted like a big boy all day, he would be able to have the toy that he had seen in the shop window. It was an expensive building set, but he would have to wait until the following weekend for it and never mention it until then.

Lisa's sister, Susan, sat to the other side of Peter. The two sisters had spoken briefly before they sat and asked how each other was doing; however, Susan's behaviour was different. She was acting cagey. Her husband, Karl, had told Lisa that they had travelled up the night before and squeezed into one of the rooms, with their two girls, over a local public house. They had all managed to get a decent night's sleep because it was a quiet place.

Lisa had noticed their strange behaviour towards each other and sensed that everything was not okay between them. They might have fallen out after an argument, but it seemed more than that. It was doubtful that Elizabeth had noticed their odd behaviour, so did it matter?

The evening get-together had got started. It had to have been the most mind-numbing party she could remember ever going to. The music was dire. The song choices were rubbish. The disc jockey looked like he had got dressed in the dark as no one would have chosen those clothes to go together on purpose. His microphone gave out intermittent high-pitched noises as he insisted on almost chewing off the top of it. It made his voice sound muffled. Nobody bothered to get up to dance and the disc jockey did not even notice. It was not her type of music and the one consolation was that it was being played at a low volume. There were no party lights of any description. It was as though no one had put any real effort into the planning. It felt more like a business meeting with Robert's associates in attendance than it did a celebration.

Elizabeth stood by Roberts's side as he knocked back the shots of malt, one after the other, with no obvious effect. She watched him as he laughed with his guests and she smiled when they smiled and laughed when they laughed.

Lisa watched Robert and noticed that he never took the time to introduce Elizabeth to any of his acquaintances or include her in their conversations. They did not attempt to talk to her either as though she were invisible or not important. She seemed oblivious to all this, so what did it matter. Robert had not spoken to either Lisa or Susan or acknowledged that they were there. Unsure if it was a deliberate act on his part, Lisa presumed that it wasn't. He was just one of those people that was full of his own self-importance. She decided that day that she did not like her mother's new husband but would pretend that she did because at least he appeared to make Elizabeth happy.

Making her excuses, Lisa said goodbye to Susan and her family. Karl saw the opportunity to announce that he thought that maybe it was time that they made tracks. He had a plausible reason to back it up. No objections were heard from Susan as they started to gather their belongings.

For a moment, Elizabeth left Robert's side to join Lisa and Susan. She looked disappointed but was her usual understanding self as she knew that it had been a long day and her grandchildren were tired. Smiling, she hugged each of them, in turn, and thanked them all for coming.

There was no immediate honeymoon for Elizabeth and Robert. He had not made any arrangements to take her somewhere warm, quiet and romantic. They were supposed to be going somewhere special later in the year. He did mention that there might be a possibility of them going on a cruise over the Christmas and New Year period. His work commitments meant that was the one time that he could make for the two of them. She knew that he was a busy man and would look forward to their getaway, but it never transpired.

Robert would attend meetings at unsociable times and sometimes he would be away from home for several days at a time. There were Harry and Eliza around for company, but Robert had advised Elizabeth not to get close to them. They were, after all, their employees and not friends.

Of course, Elizabeth had partaken in the occasional tipple; however, nothing ever to excess. She had an endless supply available to her with a wine cellar full of red, white and rose. In the past she had seen several friends and some family members taken at an early age because of the demons that escort the drink. Every single one of them had thought that they had it under control until realising that, in fact, they could not go a day without any alcohol passing their lips. She would need to monitor her intake because at times that is all she would have for company.

Chapter Three
Moving On

Crowds of tourists from different parts of the globe arrived at the Lake District every day in their droves. The cold damp weather was never a deterrent. Most of the local village shops displayed camping and walking equipment and to some of the visitors it was vital that they peered through every window. Cafes, restaurants and bed & breakfasts occupied most of the other premises and were kept busy with the passing trade.

Lisa steered Peter's pushchair along the narrow paths and around the flow of disorientated sightseers as she made her way home. She was forced to stop every few steps and it was frustrating as she waited for other pedestrians to move along or pass her. Goosebumps emerged over her body as the raindrops started to fall. Albeit light, they had both left home without either their umbrellas or raincoats, regardless of the cautionary weather forecast on the news that morning.

Despite the rain, a tall man chose to unfold an ordnance survey map several feet ahead of them. He was dressed in a coordinating waterproof jacket and trousers with a cumbersome rucksack on his back. In his well-worn hiking boots, he stood to the centre of the path, causing an obstruction as he held out his map. He seemed oblivious to those around him as he continued to walk towards Lisa and Peter. A young loved-up couple were forced to jump out of his way, but they just sniggered and took shelter in a shop doorway.

Lisa found herself surrounded and was not able to move. She began to feel agitated as a group of people stood close behind her, whilst some of the passing vehicles clipped the edge of the kerb as they drove by. She leant forward and feigned a dry cough. "Excuse me," she began.

Peter glanced up at her with a look of anticipation. He looked sleepy from the previous day's outing with his grandmother.

The man made no response nor indicated that he had heard her and appeared to be unaware that Lisa's words were aimed at him. He tilted his head to one side and continued to analyse his map.

Lisa called out to the man. This time she said it louder so that she could be heard above the noise of the traffic.

The man continued to remain in a world of his own. He did not answer, but without warning, he stopped walking and stood in front of Peter's pram.

Seeing his opportunity, Peter kicked out with both of his legs at the same time. The front of his shoes struck the man's shins.

The man stumbled and crumpled his map. "Ouch," he hollered. "What the…?" He managed to stop himself from swearing when he noticed that it was a young child that had lashed out at him. Looking at Peter, he frowned. "You need to get that child under control," the man remarked with an accent that Lisa could not place.

Peter put his hand over his mouth in an attempt to disguise his amusement. He thought it was funny that the man's eyebrows met in the middle and were separated by a single deep frown line.

"Really?" Lisa took a deep breath before she continued. There was a hint of cynicism to her tone, "Our apologies, but I did try to get your attention. You clearly didn't hear me."

Ignoring Lisa's explanation, the man raised his glare and looked at the top of her head. "And I don't suppose you will bother to chastise the little brat."

Some of the people behind Lisa were growing impatient and began pushing against her, while others waited for a lull in the traffic and walked into the road to pass her. She could hear some of them cursing under their breath.

"Bloody prams!"

"Hasn't that child got a pair of legs?"

"Some people seem to have all day!"

Lisa stopped herself from giving them all her middle finger and smiled through gritted teeth whilst she remained calm. Nevertheless, she felt unhappy with the man's rude behaviour and gave him her response, "Yes... but not here where everyone is watching. I will have words with the little 'brat' when I get him home."

She reached forward to stroke Peter's hair. It was her way of reassuring him that she was not cross with him and everything would be okay. "And in future I might suggest that you bother to look where you are going," she added.

The man made eye contact with Lisa. His behaviour changed and he became serene. The sockets around his eyes had darkened. She had seen that mask before and on more than one occasion. She surmised his impending demise but wondered how it would happen. "It's time that you went home, back to Beechwood, Lisa. It's where you belong." He smiled, nodded his head and stepped sideways into the road, but his timing was amiss as a car struck him.

The horrified driver's arms were out straight as she gripped the steering wheel and revealed the whites of her knuckles. Her washed out face was a clear indication that she had not expected the man to step out in front of her. The screeching brakes timed to the same instant as the thudding sound of the man's legs being fractured. His body soared through the air before he landed across the rear window of the car. An unmistakeable crack could be heard as his head struck the tempered glass. A steady flow of blood from his ears, nose and a large open wound on his scalp trickled down over the car and onto the road. The rain tried to rinse it away.

The sound of hysterical screaming followed, and the traffic came to a standstill in both directions. Despite the heavier rain, it did not stop curious folk from winding down their car windows and hanging out to get a better look. Onlookers appeared to exit the shops in a speedy manner and gather together in small groups to check on the situation. Most of them were unable to help and only got in the way. They nudged each other and pointed at the accident as though it were some type of spectator sport. Others saw it as an opportunity to take a photograph of themselves, looking either glum, shocked or smiling with the scene of the accident behind them.

Lisa stood and watched as the madness continued to unfold. She was puzzled. *How did he know what my name is and the name of the village where I grew up?* She caught sight of the black shadow in the road, to the side of the car that had sent the man flying through the air, but she needed to get Peter away from the collision as he had already seen too much. She put her head down and continued on her way.

Standing outside her apartment door, Lisa leant forward to unfasten the belt clip on Peter's pushchair. He had long since outgrown it. The belt was snug around his waist and the front of his scuffed shoes would, more often than not, scrape along the ground. The fastener was stiff and would involve using some force which would result in gouging out a small piece of skin from somewhere on her hand. That occasion was to be no different as she placed the smarting finger into her mouth.

Shuffling his bottom to the front of his pushchair, Peter moved himself forward and jumped out. He stood to the side of Lisa whilst she rummaged about in her pockets and looked for the door key. It wasn't there. Opening the zip to her handbag, she peered inside and was greeted by an array of essential items. After shuffling her hand about amongst the bag's contents, she bent down and tipped it out onto the floor. The key wasn't there. She looked over towards the door of her new neighbour where a mound of filled black bin bags had accumulated to the side of their door and had started to extend along the corridor. A pungent smell accompanied the waste. She shook her head and rolled her eyes upwards. Collecting her items from the floor, she put them back into her bag before she discovered that the key was in her trouser pocket, the first place that she had looked. She inserted it into the keyhole and unlocked the door.

Like a miniature soldier, Peter stood to attention with his back against the door and held it open for Lisa. Water from his wet hair trickled down over his face and his clothes dripped onto the floor. He saluted, like one of the guards at Buckingham Palace, as she folded up the pushchair and carried it inside. He closed the door behind them.

Looking around, Lisa marvelled at how tidy the place looked. The neatness would not last, however, as Peter took off his wet shoes and left them on the floor in the same place where they fell. He dashed over to his toy box and emptied its contents onto the floor. He would play by himself for hours and would only need his mother's attention if he needed food, drink or to let her know that he was making a trip to the toilet.

Lisa grabbed a couple of towels from out of the bathroom and placed one of them over the top of Peter's head. He took this as his cue to strip down to his underpants before he rubbed the towel through his hair. She wrapped her towel around her head; however, she kept her wet clothes on.

The postman had made his morning delivery while they were out and he had left most of the mail sticking out of her letterbox, as usual, allowing anyone passing her door to help themselves if they felt that way inclined. Pulling it out, Lisa picked up the remainder, of what looked like junk mail, from the doormat. She thumbed through it. There was nothing of importance. There was a takeaway menu, gardening services leaflet (she sniggered), new windows and door offer and a 'to the occupier' letter.

Lisa's attention was drawn to the sound of a raised voice which could be heard coming from the new neighbour's apartment. A young lady and her daughter had not long since moved in. She believed the young lady's name to be Lauren; however, no formal introductions were ever made. She did not know what the little girl's name was. Lauren appeared to be pleasant and would smile when she said, hello. It was not her voice that Lisa could hear, however, but that of a worked-up young man. She presumed that it was Lauren's boyfriend, Josh. His visits had become frequent and he would stay overnight. She had heard Lauren call out his name during the night. The connecting walls were thin!

Peter did not appear to have noticed the shouting. He continued to lay on his stomach whilst he played with his Star Wars action figures and simulated the necessary sound effects with his voice.

Throwing the junk mail straight into the recycling basket, Lisa made a start on the dirty laundry that was overflowing the sides of the wash basket. She pulled out the coloured items, turned them inside out and started loading them into the washing machine. Josh's voice quietened and it got louder again as he began to pace across the floor, but he would often sound too muffled which made it difficult to make anything definite out. The shouting stopped and there was a slamming of their door. The walls of Lisa's apartment shook.

Rushing over to her door, Lisa imagined that Josh would have an enraged expression on his face. She looked through the spyhole and manoeuvred her head so that she was able to get a better view of him. His footsteps echoed, as though he was stamping his feet down on purpose, as he walked up and down the full length of the corridor. There was something about him that made her feel uncomfortable, but she was not sure what it was. He continued to work himself up into a frenzy, swearing out loud and throwing his arms out in front of him as he forced himself to repeat the whole argument, word for word. The stomping stopped. He was standing outside Lisa's apartment and looking down towards the gap at the bottom of her door. *Shit, does he know that I'm watching him?* She remained still and continued to look at him. His face grew larger until it was just a close-up of an eyeball that was visible through the spyhole. He began to back away, but not before he had hit the side of his fist against the door. Her heart raced. She gulped out loud when she realised that the door was unlocked. Pushing the bolt on, she retreated as though the door was transparent and he could see her every move.

Walking back over to the washing machine, Lisa continued to sort the laundry. She turned the machine on. "Damn," she cursed after realising that she had forgotten to put a wash capsule in with the load. *That damn Josh has got me all flustered. I'll need to do that load again.*

When Peter heard Lisa curse, he looked over at her. He pulled a throw from off the back of the sofa, wrapped it around himself and continued to play.

A muffled thumping noise could be heard coming from the corridor, but it was nothing like the previous sound of Josh's footsteps. Lisa looked through the spyhole. She had expected to see him standing there with his angry face staring right back at her as he prepared to break down her door. *What possible grievances could he have with me though?* But he was no longer standing outside her door. He appeared to be taking out any remaining frustration on the pile of bin bags that were outside on the corridor. The heap was no more as he continued to kick at the pile until the bags burst open. Their contents spilt out over the floor and a pile of soiled nappies emerged from beneath. He had disturbed the flies. There were too many to count.

Why's the apartment next door so quiet while that Josh carries on acting like a mad man? I wonder if he's done something to Lauren and her daughter. Oh no, he might have seriously hurt them or worse still, killed them. Should I call around and investigate or ring the police and leave it to them? Josh had made Lisa feel uncomfortable in her own home and she did not like it. *But, do I really want to be getting myself involved? Anyway, what excuse could I use if I called around to check, especially when he's still hanging around outside? Hopefully, it'll all blow over and he'll come to his senses and calm down.*

A gradual brightness shone on an area of the corridor as the door of the next apartment was opened with noticeable caution. A figure stood in its opening and blocked out part of that light. A large shadow appeared across the floor. A smaller shadow emerged and kept close by. Though they were out of sight, Lisa felt a sense of relief wash over her. *Thank goodness that Lauren and her daughter are still alive.* There would be no crime scene investigation tape fixed across the door, blocking access to that apartment and no chalk lines would be drawn around where the bodies had been found.

Josh's tantrum stopped as his attention was drawn to whoever was standing in the doorway. What had been the reason for his outburst? It couldn't have been anything serious or Lauren wouldn't be allowing him to set foot back inside. There would not be any further shouting or bad behaviour that day. Like a chastised child, he lowered his head as he made his way back inside the apartment. He dragged his feet as though he knew that he was about to be made to sit on the naughty step. The light and shadows disappeared as the door closed with as much care as it had been opened.

The landline telephone began to ring. Its piercing tone distracted Peter. He ran to answer it. "Hello... hello," he said before looking up at Lisa.

"Thank you, sweetheart." Lisa reached to take the handset from Peter's hand. Its cord was twisted. "Hello." Smiling, she realised how silly they must both have sounded to whoever was on the other end of the line.

"Lisa, it's me... your mum. Err... I was just checking that you were in before I called round for a coffee." Elizabeth sounded out of breath.

"Yes, we're in. Well obviously, as I've just answered the phone." Lisa paused before she asked, "Is everything okay? You don't usually ring to check first."

"Yes, everything's fine. I'll see you both soon." The telephone line went dead.

Standing next to the telephone, Lisa put the handset onto its cradle before she drifted off into one of her trances. She thought about Pauline, a previous neighbour, who had lived next door before Lauren and her daughter had moved in. Pauline was a quiet middle-aged lady who had lived there by herself and appeared to enjoy her own company. Lisa had only heard her when she was singing at the top of her voice while vacuuming to either a Rod Stewart song or a Cliff Richard number; however, much to Lisa's disappointment, she returned home from work one day to discover that Pauline had moved out without taking the time to say goodbye.

In the first couple of weeks, Lauren and her daughter were quiet and the perfect tenants, but it started to deteriorate when Josh showed up. It was not any one major incident. It was a lot of little annoying things that built up. Lisa recalled that the disturbances all seemed to begin when he was trying to make it up with Lauren and as a way of an apology for his irrational behaviour. Animals were not allowed inside the apartment block, but Lisa had passed him on the corridor and noticed the puppy that was tucked away inside his jacket with its big brown eyes peeking out. She pretended that she had not seen it and did not trouble herself to speak to him.

As cute as the puppy was, it was not a pleasant experience having to listen to its whining at night. As the night grew longer and it got quieter outside, the puppy's whimpering appeared to get louder. It was never determined if Lisa's new neighbours had gone out and left it alone in unfamiliar surroundings, were ignoring it or were able to sleep through the noise, because not one of them bothered to get up from their bed to console the poor creature. The puppy was not there for the night, it was there to stay. It must have started to feel settled, however, as the whining died down until it stopped after several nights.

Josh did not go out to work, well to do a conventional job. To earn himself a bit of easy money, he would turn his hand to anything. It was doubtful that the taxman saw his cut of any of the cash from those illegal activities. The smell of cannabis, from Josh's roll-ups, would permeate through into Lisa's apartment whenever he was around, which made her and Peter feel sick.

Lauren was a stay-at-home mum. She had set up some sort of animal day care, which involved looking after other people's pets during the day while they went out to work or for others when they went away on holiday. The barking and the sound of incessant scratching down the connecting wall was annoying and when you combined that with another one of their ventures—an overnight babysitting service, it resulted in crying infants during the night. It appeared that the neighbours would manage to sleep through the din and would emerge the following day unaffected.

After Josh returned from one of his hunts, there would be birds of the larger varieties hanging upside down outside one of Lauren's windows. Did they ever eat what he killed? When he brought the birds back, he would tie string around their legs and hang them from a number of hooks. You could see them when you looked up from the road below. It was a sickening sight to see their glorious wingspan spread out. On occasion these lifeless bodies would become a frenzied banquet for other wild birds to feast on. It puzzled Lisa as to what he did with the remains, when there was not much left for him to make a meal with, and what he did with all those cats that he brought back some nights, crammed inside a cage.

The sound of the doorbell put a stop to Lisa's thoughts. Of course, she knew who was there, but felt it necessary to have a peek through the spyhole to check. She opened the door and was greeted by a flushed Elizabeth. "Hi, Mum. Come in." Lisa moved to one side so that she could pass and looked out onto the corridor. There were no other signs of life. She closed the door and locked it behind her.

One of Elizabeth's knees clicked as she bent down to take off her shoes. "It's busy out there, already," she said, in between wheezing, as she struggled to breathe. She started to cough, a dry hack, which did little to assist in her relief. Hanging up her jacket on her usual hook, she reached into its left-hand pocket and took out her reliever. She inhaled.

Lisa waited as she wanted to make sure that Elizabeth was going to be all right and that she was not going to have another asthma attack.

Elizabeth caught her breath.

"I know, it will be today. Don't you find that it's always buzzing on a weekend? That's why I go out first thing in the morning and grab what I need from the shop."

Elizabeth was still recovering as she made her way towards the kitchen area. She waved at Peter and he raised his hand in response. "I'll make us both a nice hot drink," she said, as she rubbed her hands together in an attempt to warm them. "You know that I like to make myself feel useful when I come around to visit." She turned on the tap and filled the kettle to its maximum line. "Did he say if he enjoyed himself yesterday?" She pointed over at Peter.

"I presume so. He's not really said very much this morning. You must have tired him out yesterday."

"He was a right little chatterbox yesterday." Elizabeth paused before she changed the subject, "There was an ambulance struggling to get through the traffic as I walked up here. It's probably still trying to get to that poor man that's laying in the road." She flicked on the kettle switch and coughed onto the back of her hand. "The poor sod looked like he'd been hit by a car. A young lady was trying to give him CPR, but it didn't look at all promising for him." She turned around to look at Lisa, who had followed her into the kitchen area. "Did you not see anything while you were out?"

With recent events taking up Lisa's thoughts, she had forgotten about the man and him being hit by that car. "No, I didn't. It must have happened after we got back. I hope that he'll be okay." She looked over at Peter, who continued to play with his toys, but he did stop for a moment when he heard his mother lying to his grandmother. It was her turn to change the subject, "Anyway, it's all happening today because next door have just had a right argument before you got here."

I know that she's hiding something because she's got guilt written all over her face. I've been able to tell since she was a little girl when she's telling me a lie. "Which side?" Elizabeth had prepared the cups and was watching over the kettle while pointing, in turn, to the apartments on the opposite sides.

"The newbies." Lisa tipped her head to one side to show Elizabeth which neighbour she was referring to. *Anyway, why should I be made to feel responsible? It was his stupid decision to side step into the road. He's a fully-grown man... correction, was. It's not like I pushed him or anything, tempted as I was.*

"Josh sounded like he was really losing his temper. Then he stormed out, slammed the door and had a major tantrum outside on the corridor. He was kicking them bin bags about. He's made a right mess." Lisa looked at the spyhole. "Then, he had the gall to punch my door."

"Really? That's strange."

"Why?" Lisa was confused as to why her mother doubted her. "Did you not see the mess outside when you got here?"

"Of course I did, you can't really miss it. I had to play hopscotch over it to get to your door and then there's that horrible smell that greets you as soon as you open the main entrance door. It seems to be getting worse every time I call around." Elizabeth waved her hand in front of her nose. "I'm only saying it's strange because I saw Lauren and her little girl about an hour ago in the village. They're going away for the weekend. Well that's what she told me anyway. They both looked so happy and really excited about it."

"Was it just Lauren and her daughter?" Lisa asked. "Are you sure that it was them?"

"Yes, definitely, they're going to stay at Lauren's mother's house." Elizabeth raised her voice as Lisa made her way to the far end of the living room. "I was a bit surprised that she was bothering to tell me because she's never really spoken to me before, but I think she was just bursting to tell someone. I helped her to put their bags into the boot. I watched them as they got into a taxi that was going to take them to the airport."

Lisa started to question herself as she stood with her ear to a glass tumbler that she had pressed against the wall of the neighbour's apartment. *Is it possible that he was having an argument with someone over the phone? After all, I only really heard the one voice and that was his.*

"Can you hear anything?" Elizabeth asked.

Lisa shook her head. "No... nothing. It's deadly quiet. Josh must have been talking to someone on the phone." *But if that is the case, then who did those two shadows belong to that I saw standing in the doorway?*

"Well at least that Josh is quiet now. Hopefully, that will be the end of that." Elizabeth reached up to grab a packet of chocolate digestives that had rolled to the back of the kitchen cupboard. Lisa joined her when she heard the teaspoons stirring inside the cups. Peter ran across when he heard the biscuit packet rustling as they were being opened. Lisa grabbed an orange juice carton from the fridge and pierced the hole in its lid with the plastic straw. As they all sat on the kitchen stools, they munched on the biscuits and slurped their drinks. Lisa and Elizabeth gave themselves a moment before they continued to chat. "Anyway, have Bev and Colin got back from their little getaway yet?"

Peter ran back to his toys, as he did not want to listen to his mother moaning about them as well.

"I've absolutely no idea. I don't think they have." Lisa had not noticed. She had been distracted with the goings-on of the new neighbours. "I'm sure I would have heard Bev if they had got back."

A young professional couple who lived to the other side of Lisa had a few months earlier welcomed a baby boy, Alan, into their lives. Bev and Colin had moved into their apartment a couple of weeks after Lisa had moved into hers. At the time, she felt blessed to have such pleasant neighbours. Up until the birth of their son, the only time that she could hear them was when they would invite their friends over for a social gathering of an evening and the sounds of their laughter could be heard coming through the connecting wall.

Colin remained a quiet man, but Bev changed into a different person when her husband went out. She was struggling with the whole parenting thing and was not patient and became louder when she was left to look after Alan by herself. Lisa knew when Colin was out. She would not need to look out of the window to check to see if his car was parked below because Bev's noise levels with Alan were confirmation.

The sounds of Alan crying for lengthy periods were of no comfort to anyone, let alone Bev, and her approaches to calm him were of no relief. When her method of shouting for him to "shut up" made the situation worse, her other technique was at first comical until it drove all within earshot slowly insane. In an effort to calm his upset, she would make strange wooing noises that would get louder until he would be forced to quieten down. These imitation orgasmic noises, which would last for long periods, would make themselves present whenever it sounded like she was about to lose control.

"The poor woman. I think that Bev's just finding it hard coping with being a mother." Elizabeth looked at Lisa as though she had expected her to feel the same. "And if making those daft noises helps to quieten him down, then that's what she needs to do. It's better than her hitting him, don't you think?"

"Yes, I suppose that you're right; nevertheless, all of my neighbours are really starting to get on my nerves. I don't want to hear what they're all doing every minute of the day and night. Any more than I would want them to hear Peter and me." Lisa looked at Elizabeth, she thought back to how her mother would stand and say nothing as she watched John carry out his punishments when she was younger.

Elizabeth felt awkward talking about other people in a derogatory way. She noticed that Lisa was anxious and gave her a half-hearted smile.

"Oh, I don't know… just ignore me. I'm in one of those moods today. It's probably down to the fact that I'm really knackered. In fact, I feel like this most days now." Lisa paused. *Come on, Lisa. You know that you've got to let her know and now seems as good a time as any.* She took a deep breath and the words came out, "There's something that I need to tell you. I've given it a lot of thought… I think that it's time that Peter and I moved on."

"Move on! Where to?" Elizabeth asked. "Despite your neighbours, I thought that you were happy here."

"I was, up until a few months ago. You know that I like my peace and quiet, but it's just not like that here any more." Lisa paused and noted the silence. "It is at the moment, but how long is that going to last? Things have changed and I just can't seem to relax. Plus, Peter

53

needs his own room. He shouldn't still be sharing with me at his age." Lisa stood up, looked over at Peter and smiled. *I know that I'm making the right decision.* "I know that he doesn't mind at the moment, but he will do, and soon. He's growing up so fast."

"You could move in with us. There's plenty of room and I know that Robert wouldn't mind." Elizabeth grew excited at the thought of them living together.

"That sounds like an excellent plan, but you and Robert are still newlyweds really. It's nearly your anniversary and you don't want us two getting under your feet. I'm planning to move out of the area and back to Beechwood," Lisa felt a tinge of guilt and found it necessary to explain her decision. "I realise that I've made friends here. I will miss all of the walking group dearly and I'll miss you, but we can still come up and visit you all. It's only a couple of hours drive away. I want Peter to see where I grew up and for him to play in Beechwood Park. I just know that it would be good for him and he's going to love it." She handed Elizabeth another biscuit. "I need to find a house with a garden so that Peter can play out in the fresh air. When I moved up here, I was on my own and only had myself to worry about. Now, I can feel Beechwood pulling me back. I need to go home."

Lisa and Elizabeth sat in silence, but Elizabeth was not able to hide her sadness. Peter joined them and stood to the side of his grandmother. He could sense her grief.

"It'll be okay, Grandma," he said, as he put his hand onto her arm and patted her.

Lisa put her apartment up for sale, but potential buyers were put off with the mess that was scattered along the corridor and by the accompanying smell. She knocked on Lauren's door to have a word with her, on different days and at various times, but no one ever answered. She informed the landlord that owned that apartment, but he made it clear that he was not interested. Every day, Lisa cleared away some of the rubbish until it was all gone. But, despite disinfecting the corridor, a persistent smell lingered.

Not a sound had been heard from Lauren's place since about the time that Elizabeth had explained to Lisa that she had seen Lauren and her daughter going away on that weekend break. Next door's landline would ring for long periods of time and on each occasion it would remain unanswered. It was obvious that someone was eager to speak to her, but not enough to bother to call around in person and take the time to knock on her door.

Several weeks had gone by. Lauren's landlord called around and knocked on her door. She had gone into arrears with her rent and was not answering the door. His attempts to shout through the letterbox to get her attention, were being ignored. The landlord tried to let himself in with his key but couldn't because the lock had been changed. He was left with no other option but to ring the police and notify them that he was about to break in.

The landlord began pacing, up and down the corridor, as he waited for the police to arrive. It was debatable, to anyone that was observing, if he was doing it to try to keep himself calm or if he was making matters worse and winding himself up.

Two young police officers arrived. One of them knocked on the door, twice, while the other stood behind him. There was no response. The door gave little resistance as it gave way against the force from the sole of one of the officer's size eleven, boots slamming against it. With the resounding noise of the wood splintering, the door crashed open and damaged both the lock and the door frame.

The smell of decomposing flesh escaped and filled every crevice of the apartment blocks corridors. A huge swarm of flies followed. Josh's body could be seen decaying on his sofa. His face was unrecognisable. He was dressed in the clothes that he had been wearing when he lost his temper that day, only several weeks earlier. He was laid down on his side, as though resting, with his head on a pile of cushions. His legs were tucked up and his arms were folded loosely in front of him.

The two officers had not expected to find a corpse when they arrived at the scene. Both of them were unprepared and it was clear from their facial expressions that neither of them had seen anything like it before in their short careers. When they were greeted by the foul smell it caused them to cover their mouths and noses, but it was too late, as both of them brought up their breakfasts.

The landlord, who did not appear to be shocked, hung back and waited within sight, along the corridor. He had found a dead body on one previous occasion and remembered that unforgettable smell of death when he approached the apartment and lifted the letterbox flap.

Upon further inspection of the apartment, the police discovered that Lauren's and her daughter's clothes were gone. There was not a trace of either of them nor any sign that they had ever lived there. When Lauren had told Elizabeth that she was going away to her mother's house to stay for the weekend, she was never going to return. Josh's belongings could be found in and amongst the neglect of his dirty clothes and the plates and cups that were scattered around the place. An unbelievable amount of mess was created in the short time that they lived there. The remains of their puppy lay on the bathroom floor and the skeletons of other animals were found piled in the bath tub.

Josh's body was removed, inside a black body bag, on a stretcher. The rumours spread fast. He died from asphyxiation, which the autopsy would later confirm.

The black shadow took two lives that day. Bloodshed was one of the easiest jobs in the world and the black shadow never tired of doing it. The first death was a simple road traffic accident and the man did not see it coming. It was simple and could have happened to anyone on his hit list.

However, the second one, Josh, he took a while longer. Long-suffering Lauren had tried to escape him for years, but he managed to find her. He had never raised a hand to her, but he was a workshy waster and would take drugs as soon as he rose from his bed. Lauren had told Josh the same story as she had told Elizabeth. He did not suspect a thing and did not even notice that she had taken all her belongings with her. It was his dealer that he had argued with on the telephone that morning. Josh owed him money and his dealer would not supply him anything else until he paid some of his mounting debt.

Josh saw the black shadow and a smaller one in the doorway and followed them back inside the apartment. There were others that were waiting inside for him, but he did not bother to count them. He thought that he was having another one of his bad trips and tried to calm himself. He went through the motions of dancing with them, tried talking to them and even offered them each a drink. They toyed with him and swayed around the room until he lost his balance, fell over and slumped onto the sofa. The smaller shadows left and disappeared into the floor. It was Josh and the black shadow that remained. Josh became weary. He laid down, closed his eyes and fell asleep. The black shadow made its move and smothered him.

Chapter Four
Alone

Fred had wondered what he was going to do with his time, to start with, when he retired. He was worried that his days would be as empty as the nights were long. He was going to try out various hobbies and pastimes while he made new friends. Golf was to be the first distraction on his list. If he found that he did not enjoy it or was no good at it and wasting his time, he would venture onto something else.

Not a day went by when Fred did not think about Peter. He was convinced that it was his voice that he had heard in the storeroom. He was willing to stake his life on it. People that knew the family would ask if Peter had turned up when they called into his shop. Each time, Fred would shake his head and say that his son was still on the missing persons list. A poster, which had faded over the years from the sunlight, was displayed on his shop door.

Fred's shop had become a bit of a tourist attraction. That was, in the main, because of the rumours that it was the source of the Ouija board that was linked to the Victoria Willis murder. The inquisitive customers were sociable, but he found that they liked to browse his stock rather than buy. Requests for Ouija boards were plentiful, but he was not a stockist and had no recollection of where he had got that particular one from.

Fred thought about tidying away the mess that was left behind from his retirement party. His guests had taken the leftover food, but they had left a few softened crisps. He would throw them out for the birds, later. He was not surprised to find empty wine bottles and glasses placed, at random, around his shop without a drop of alcohol in sight.

The bell above the shop door struggled to ping as the latest customers entered. Fred looked up and watched as a group of five young men walked in. It was impossible to tell them apart. They looked immaculate, dressed from head to toe in black. Each had hair as dark as ebony. They were slim in build and were all the same height. Their colourless complexions emphasised what looked like, smudged eye make-up. One by one, they entered the shop, moving in an eerie regimental manner as they leant forward as though being pulled in by an unseen force. They moved slower than their pace would suggest as their feet appeared not to make contact with the floor. Each of them was staring down until the last one made his way through the door. This young man put his head up and looked at Fred. His eyes were black, like empty sockets, with no obvious iris or white to the eye. It was instinct that made Fred look away, but it was not out of fear as he felt calm.

For the first time that day, the sun had broken through the clouds. It glared through the shop window. Fred unfastened the top button of his shirt and ran his index finger along the inside of his collar while he pulled it away from his skin. His fingernail was a welcome relief to the itching around his neckline.

After wedging open the shop door, Fred turned around to discover that his customers were not browsing the remaining stock and were sitting on the floor in a circle. Their legs were crossed, heads bowed, and arms outstretched in front of them, while they held hands. Shuffling his feet around them, Fred walked back behind his counter. He took off his cardigan, placed it over the back of his chair and brushed away several noticeable flakes of dandruff. He pulled out the chair, with care, as he did not want to disturb his customers.

It was customary for Fred to prepare himself a packed lunch each morning and that day was no different. Although there was food and drink at his party, only alcohol had passed his lips. It was normal for him to eat his meals at set times, but he did not feel hungry that day. It was later than usual, and he felt that it was necessary for him to eat. His lunch bag contents were the same each day, a dry ham sandwich in brown granary which would be followed by a packet of plain crisps and a banana. Every day, he would eat them in that order.

Biting into the sandwich, Fred began to chew, but the bread was dry, and he felt thirsty after one mouthful.

He licked his lips to try to moisten them. A cup of tea would follow his food, but he had decided that he was going to have that cuppa during his lunch instead. It was, after all, the day of his retirement and his routine would need to change. Noticing that bread crumbs had fallen onto his trousers, he flicked them off with the back of his hand, got to his feet and made his way to the storeroom.

Fred stopped in the doorway and looked towards the sink. *It was Peter's voice that I heard. I know that it wasn't my imagination.* He thought about the entity. *But where was that thing trying to take me?* He looked down at the fresh scars that were on the underside of his hand.

Putting an already used teabag into his stained cup, Fred waited for the kettle to boil. He watched as the steam rose into the air and evaporated. His customers had not made a sound. He popped his head around the door. The five young men were still seated on the floor and had not moved. *It must be some kind of spiritual gathering. Perhaps they're meditating, but why have they chosen my shop to do it in? It would have been nice for them to say hello.* He decided that he would ask them when he went back through.

Pouring the water into the cup, the vapour hit Fred in his face and steamed up his glasses that were perched on the end of his nose. His sugar supply was gone, and the milk was sour, so his tea would have to be an unsweetened black one.

Fred meant to cough as he walked into the front of the shop. It was a wasted attempt, however, as nothing it seemed would distract the five young men from their business. He carried his cup with care, so as not to spill his drink. Blowing into his cup to cool his tea, he took a sip before putting it on top of a pizza takeaway leaflet. It had been posted through his letterbox with the rest of the junk mail and there appeared to be more than usual that day. He pondered on how he might broach the subject of what the young men were doing, but each question he mulled over, in his mind, seemed somehow intrusive, so he did not bother and took another bite of his sandwich.

Picking up an empty cardboard box, Fred placed it onto his chair and continued to pack away some of the smaller fragile items in bubble wrap and newspaper. The sounds of rustling and the popping of air balls did not appear to disturb the young men from their meditation. The charity shop across the road was to benefit from his generosity. After filling up another box, he would either walk across the road to drop it off or Linda would call in to collect it.

A small wooden box, an interesting piece with an intriguing pattern chiselled on the lid, caught Fred's attention. He put it up to his mouth and blew. Globules of spittle flew out and landed on the box and on the underside of his wrist. He disturbed some of the dust from within its carving. A few feet away to his left, a small piece of paper flew out from underneath his till. It floated in the air, for a moment, before it landed on the floor. *What could it be?* Placing the box down, he balanced himself with his hand against the counter, bent his knees, with care, and picked up the piece of paper. Both of his knee joints clicked in protest. After straightening back up, he turned the piece of paper over and placed it onto the palm of his hand. He was taken aback by what he saw. It was an old photograph of his son, Peter, when he was a new-born baby and he was being cradled in the arms of his late wife, Katherine.

In hindsight it was obvious, but at the time Fred had not had the slightest idea because his excitement at becoming a father had been overwhelming. Katherine looked so unhappy on that photograph. Her smile appeared false and her eyes were filled with sadness and yet, Peter looked such a cheerful baby. Holding the photograph against his chest, he closed his eyes for a moment.

For months after Peter's birth, Katherine had suffered with post-natal depression which resulted in her taking her own life. Fred did not remember her complaining, although her demeanour had been quieter during that time. It took him years to stop holding himself responsible. After her passing, he did not want to settle down with anyone else and he never looked at another woman in that way.

Fred opened his eyes and took another look at the photograph before he placed it into the pocket of his cardigan. Lifting the cardboard box from the chair and onto the counter, he sat and looked out of the window. He watched as the local folk went about their business. *It's strange that nobody is stopping to chat or even taking the time to look up at each other.* Every one of them appeared to be caught up in their own world and unaware of what was going on around them. *How odd that there's not one familiar face amongst any of them.* Picking up his sandwich, Fred put it to his mouth and was about to take another bite when he noticed that he was alone. The group of young men was no longer seated on the floor. The shop door was not propped open. The bell above the door had not rung out and he had not noticed them pass the window. Putting down the sandwich, he went to check in the storeroom. It was empty and the back door was locked, bolted and had two boxes propped against it.

It felt like only a couple of minutes had gone by when Fred returned to the front of the shop, yet the village was in darkness and deserted. Every shop within sight appeared closed. There was light from the street lamps and a single bulb that shone from the ceiling inside his own shop. He locked and bolted the shop door while he tried to recollect where the last few hours had gone.

Sitting on his chair, Fred pushed his sandwich to one side and opened the crisp packet. He still was not hungry, but thought it was best that he tried to eat. Putting one of the crisps into his mouth, he attempted to bite it, but there was no crunch. He pulled the softened crisp out of his mouth and put it to his nose. There was no smell. He pushed his glasses up the bridge of his nose and held the packet out in front of him and inspected it. The crisps had not exceeded the best before date. Turning his head, he caught sight of his sandwich edging its way along the counter. It was mouldy and there were numerous maggots trying to wriggle their way out and he noted that his banana was black and half its original size. Picking up a waste paper basket, he pushed his lunch across the counter and threw it inside.

Fred had expected his reflection to be prominent, but it looked like it was fading, as he looked out of the window. The shoppers appeared to have made their way home. It was usual, in the evening, for people to dine out or go to one of the public houses. Laughter would sound out along the road and on occasion it was known for the locals to finish their night with a punch-up, but Beechwood was silent.

Chapter Five
Betrayal

Peter managed to sleep, despite the pushchairs squeaking wheels and him being jolted about as Lisa pushed him through the village. His eyelids were pink and swollen from being upset and dried up tears had left salty streaks down his flushed cheeks. Lisa did not want to wipe them away as she did not want to waken him.

The cold air felt brisk and was the probable reason as to why the village was quiet. The locals appeared to be the only ones that were about as they made a dash to get their essential groceries before the onslaught of sightseers arrived.

During the night, Peter had disturbed both himself and Lisa on a number of occasions. Whilst he was sleeping, he had cried out during another series of night terrors. She had jumped up out of her bed on each occasion to quieten him and stroked his face while she whispered reassuring words into his ear. The familiarity of her calming voice helped, and she continued until he was still again. She would listen to his gentle breathing, exhale an audible sigh of relief and wish that she could take his nightmares away.

Something was puzzling Lisa about the previous night. *I put Peter's dummy down on top of the chest of drawers when I went to bed. He's only got one and it wasn't on there this morning. It was out of his reach. He didn't have it when I got out of bed to calm him, but it was there by the time I laid back down and looked over at him. He wouldn't have had time to jump up out of bed, make a grab for it and then jump back into bed and all without making a noise. I'm sure that he was asleep. So how did it find its way into his mouth?* She shook her head. *Early night, tonight, for me, I'm tired and overthinking things.*

To Peter, the explanation was obvious. He had overheard what his grandmother had said to his mother yesterday. "When are you going to take that dummy from him, Lisa? Just throw it in the bin when he's not looking. He's too big for it. He doesn't need it. Look at his teeth, they've grown crooked." Well she was wrong. What did she know? He did need it and he was going hide it, so only he knew where to find it.

In the bedroom, the lighting was dim from Peter's night light. He had peeked over at Lisa as she entered the room, put his dummy on top of the chest of drawers and climbed into her bed. It was out of her hands and he knew its exact location. He could not sleep, so he pretended that he was having one of his bad dreams. He had hoped that she would give in and let him have his dummy because she was too tired to resist, but she jumped out of bed and began fussing over him. The

68

dummy never entered his mouth. His initial plan had failed, but his back-up plan, he knew for sure, would not. Pretending to fall asleep, he felt her rise from the side of his bed and saw his opportunity. He squinted, as he needed confirmation that she was not watching. Remaining still, he focussed all of his attention towards the top of the chest of drawers. The dummy wobbled before it rose into the air and he watched as it soared towards him. He opened his mouth. The dummy slowed and landed, plugging the gap.

The general store was further along, one turn to the right and about thirty paces. Lisa turned the corner, looked ahead and noticed a familiar face. It was Susan, her sister. Lisa stopped. *What's she doing here? It's strange that Mum didn't mention that she was coming up to visit. Why all the secrecy? Maybe she wanted to surprise us.*

Susan looked excited as she paced the path before she stopped to look at her reflection in a shop window. She tidied her hair with her fingers, brushing it forward so that it fell over the front of her shoulders, and pulled a pouting expression as though blowing herself a kiss.

Susan must be waiting for someone. Karl and their girls must be inside the shop. I'll go and say hello to them. Lisa's ex-boyfriend, William Oates, hurried past Lisa. She had not seen him for a long time. The sleeve of his jacket brushed against her arm. She would recognise Bill from any angle and the unmistakeable scent of his aftershave, but it was apparent that he had not seen her. *Should I shout out to him?* She decided against it and stepped back, put her head down, but kept her eyes up. He began waving at someone who must have been standing somewhere near Susan.

Lisa counted to ten and leant forward over Peter and between the handles of his pushchair. She expected to see Bill's wife, Gillian, but someone else was embracing him. At first, Lisa was not able to work out who it was. *Where's Susan gone?* Her eyes widened. She could not believe what she was seeing. She bit her lip as she watched Bill and Susan kissing.

Wanting to run at her, Lisa felt the urge to rip out Susan's hair, but they weren't children any more. Those days were long gone or so she had thought. *Of all the millions of men on this planet, why did she have to choose Bill? What's she playing at? She's already got a loving family of her own.* The clinch seemed endless, but she could not stop herself from watching until the two of them stopped. Bill wiped the lipstick from around his mouth with a tissue and disappeared inside the shop.

Seconds later, Karl pulled up to the side of Susan in his car. She climbed into the front passenger seat, slammed the door and put on her seat belt. It was obvious that he was unaware of the recent lust fuelled embrace as he leant over to kiss his wife. *What would have happened if he'd turned up only moments earlier? Damn, I wish he bloody had done. The devious bitch.*

Karl drove past Lisa in second gear. Stacey and Jayne were sitting on the back seat and looking forward through the windscreen. Not one of them appeared to notice Lisa, but she stepped back and put her head down to be certain. When she was sure that the car was out of sight, she continued on her way.

Bill exited the shop with a smile across his face. A copy of the local newspaper was rolled up and tucked beneath his arm and a blue and white striped plastic bag, bulging with fresh fruit and vegetables, dangled from his clenched hand. The bag handles stretched and defied the odds of breakage. Lisa stood in front of him to block his path.

"Lisa," Bill said. His smugness was replaced with a wide-eyed expression. "What a lovely surprise." Wondering if she had seen his embrace with Susan, he paused. "It's been a long time. How are you?"

Finding it hard to conceal her disappointment, Lisa visualised herself grabbing Bill by his throat and kneeing him in his scrotum while, at the same time, laughing like a hysterical maniac. Feigning a smile, she did not respond and moved to one side to allow him to pass. She had decided to claim ignorance and would wait to see if he would offer her a full confession.

Standing to the side of Peter's pushchair, Bill placed his bag onto the ground. He stuffed the rolled-up newspaper inside the bag, tied the handles together and propped it against one of the wheels. "Anyway, you certainly look well." He held out his arms and hoped that Lisa might give him a hug.

Lisa was not sure if Bill was joking or trying to be nice. She had managed to put a hairbrush through her greasy hair that morning, but had not attempted to apply moisturiser, let alone make-up. "Yes, it's been a while," she responded. "You remembered my name." She pretended to chuckle. As the two of them embraced, she could smell Susan's perfume lingering on him. It was doing battle with his aftershave. She pushed him away. She wanted to cry but would not allow herself to. "And I'm really good thanks. This little monkey keeps me on my toes." She pointed at Peter. "Anyway, how are you?"

"Yeah, I'm doing okay." Bill and Lisa watched Peter as he continued to sleep. "Is this your little boy or are you minding him for someone?" he asked.

Lisa tried to do the maths in her head. *How long is it since I last saw him? Has Susan not bothered to tell him that he's a daddy? Maybe it's because they haven't been together long.* "Yes, he's my little boy," she confirmed. "His name's Peter. I've named him after his grandfather."

"Oh wow... congratulations. You did well. He looks a right little cracker." Bill gulped and smiled.

Lisa looked at Bill. She found it difficult not to frown. *Wow, he hasn't even considered for one minute that Peter might actually be his son. Maybe he thinks that I was sleeping with someone else at the time of conception. He's actually judging me by his own standards. Does he think that I was the one that was putting myself about?* To avoid saying anything that she would later regret, she bit her lip.

"Do you want me to stand here and mind Peter for you, while you pop in and do your shop?" Bill appeared unaware of Lisa's state of mind as he continued to look at Peter.

"Thanks that would be great, if you're not in a rush to be anywhere else." Lisa strolled inside the shop. She was not sure how long she would be able to keep up with the pretence.

Bill wanted to get a better look at Lisa's son. He pulled Peter's cover down, away from his face and tucked it underneath his chin. Noticing that his fringe was close to his eyes, he brushed it, with care, to one side with his fingertips. "There we go young man. We don't want that poking you in your eyes, do we?" But Peter's fringe started to fall back over his forehead. Bill leant forward and said, "This is just between the two of us, mate, but I really think that your mummy needs to get you to the hairdressers and get you a haircut."

Peter opened his eyes and looked at Bill. Without blinking, he continued to stare at him. He would not stop until he succeeded in making Bill feel uncomfortable and got him to move away.

"Hi there, little man. I'm sorry, I didn't mean to waken you." Bill felt light-headed and staggered to one side. To steady himself, he reached and grabbed the handle of the pushchair, but he missed it and stumbled. He felt an urge to sit down as a cold sweat swept over him. Swaying, he walked towards the shop door and managed to find his resting place on its step before his legs gave way. Disturbed by his weakness, he remained seated until his dizziness had passed. Peter, who was content with his accomplishment, closed his eyes and fell into a peaceful sleep.

Standing in the far corner of the shop, Lisa was trying to work out what it was that she needed to buy. She had forgotten as she was distracted by thoughts of betrayal. Continuing to walk down each aisle, she scratched her head as though it helped her to concentrate. *Should I tell Bill that Peter is his son? Is he in love with Susan? How long's it been going on?*

Lisa was staring at a packet of toilet rolls when she got distracted by Bill as he called out her name through the shop doorway. "Lisa… are you okay?" He was on his feet and looking concerned as he waited for her to respond.

"Yes, I'm coming." Lisa reached up and grabbed that same packet of toilet rolls. She made her way towards the checkout. *Whatever it was that I've come in for will just have to wait until later. I'll probably remember what I need as soon as I step through my front door.*

An elderly lady, who appeared to be happy with her lot in life, greeted Lisa from behind the cash register. Lisa rummaged through her bag, pulled out her purse, counted out the correct change, thanked the lady and left.

"Not heard a sound from him," Bill said, which was true as Peter had not uttered a word. "He did wake up for a short time, but he nodded off again." He looked at Lisa's obvious lack of groceries. "Did you manage to get everything that you needed?"

"No, not exactly." Lisa shrugged and curled her top lip at one side. "I forgot what I needed as soon as I walked into the shop." *How am I supposed to explain to him that my head is full of him and Susan kissing?* "Oh well, it is what it is. I'll just have to come back into the village when I've remembered."

Bill had noticed that Lisa looked flustered. He had not seen her like that before. "Do you want to go for a coffee?" He pointed to a café that was further up the road, where the outside sign blocked part of the path. "Whatever you needed might come back to you while you're not thinking about it." He put his hand on her shoulder with a gentle, yet reassuring, grip. "Go on... my treat." He winked. "It certainly looks like you could do with one. Perhaps even something a bit stronger, that's if it wasn't so early in the day." He picked up his shopping with one hand and put his other hand onto one of the handles of the pushchair. "We could even treat ourselves to a piece of cake, if you fancy it."

"That'd be lovely." Lisa followed Bill as he manoeuvred Peter's pushchair towards the café. They did not speak. *I could easily fall into that family life routine with Bill. He seems such a natural. If only he wasn't sleeping with my sister.*

The delicious aromas of fresh coffee greeted them as the three of them entered the café. Lisa took the handles of Peter's pushchair from Bill and found them a table away from the automatic door, which would open every time someone walked by. She pushed one of the four chairs to one side and positioned the pushchair in its place, so that she could keep an eye on Peter.

Bill walked up to the counter and joined the back of the queue. There were two people in front of him. One lady was waiting for her drinks to be served and the other lady was placing her order.

Placing the packet of toilet rolls and Bill's shopping onto one of the chairs, Lisa took off her coat and draped it over the back of her chair. She was cold but would take her coat off when she was indoors after being told numerous times as a child that she 'wouldn't feel the benefit outside' if she didn't. She sat and placed her handbag beneath the table, putting it between her feet.

Bill had not bothered to ask Lisa what she would like to drink as the two of them had shared many times together while they chatted over coffee. He did not feel that it was necessary, and he doubted that her preference would have changed.

The café's available drinks were written, in chalked calligraphy styled writing, on a large blackboard that was mounted on the wall behind the counter. Bill knew what he was going to order, but he found it necessary to read the choices that were available while he waited to be served. There was a possibility that he may order something different; however, it was doubtful.

There were two young ladies working behind the counter and both of them were wearing hideous Christmas jumpers. One of them was polite as she took the orders. Her name badge displayed Samantha. She was a cheerful character who greeted everyone as though she knew and saw them every day. "Good morning and what can I get you?" she asked Bill.

Bill placed his order, but the noise of the coffee machine as it frothed and churned made it difficult for Samantha to hear him. She leant forward and screwed up her face as though that helped her to hear what he was saying. He repeated his order, but louder, and fumbled about inside his trouser pocket as he tried to chase around some loose change. She pressed the buttons on her till, took his money and passed the receipt onto the other barista who was making the refreshments. This lady was not wearing a name badge. She made no attempts to communicate, appeared bedraggled and gave the impression she would rather be somewhere else, anywhere but work.

Bill had remembered what it was that Lisa liked to drink. She looked over at him and saw that a large cappuccino, with a chocolate dusting on top, was being prepared for her. *I wonder if he's ever bought Susan a coffee.*

Feeling jealous, Lisa pictured Bill and Susan together. The two of them were naked and making love on her bed. When they heard her walk into the room they stopped, looked over at her and began to laugh. Lisa walked towards them and raised the bread knife that had been hidden behind her back. Bill tried to escape, but she managed to stab him in his back and twisted it before she pulled it out. He fell onto the bed and his face hit the pillow. Susan screamed out some sort of an apology, but Lisa thrust the knife into her throat and listened as Susan gargled on her own blood. Lisa continued to stab them both in turn, over and over again, until silence prevailed.

Lisa's thoughts were deflected when a staff member tripped and a tray that was piled with crockery and cutlery flew through the air. Each piece either smashed or clattered and laid scattered across the floor. It was fortunate for him that no customers were sitting in that particular area of the cafe.

The café fell silent. Seated and queuing customers stopped their conversations mid-sentence. Samantha stopped taking her order and the other barista paused from making the coffee. Everybody in the café turned to look to see what the commotion was. Peter, however, stirred for a moment before he continued with his sleep. Lisa felt a tinge of sympathy for the man as his crimson complexion grew darker by the second. She looked away.

Bill enjoyed a good quality coffee, but Lisa could not remember what his preference was or if he took sugar. She guessed it would be a flat white. Walking towards her, he carried the tray with both hands while his tongue poked out and rested to the side of his bottom lip. He placed the tray onto the table and said, "I have yet to manage to get one of these damn trays back to the table without spilling at least one of the drinks." Pausing, he sighed before he continued, "I just don't understand why they feel the need to fill the cups all the way up to the rim."

It was not the first time that Lisa had heard Bill say that and word-for-word. She felt the urge to laugh but stopped herself. "Thank you." She reached to take her coffee from the tray. Some of the froth had seeped over the sides. Putting her drink onto the table, she wiped the mess with a paper napkin and took a sip.

"You're welcome. I didn't get anything for Peter. I didn't know what he liked," Bill said as he retrieved his flat white coffee. "Oh no." He looked at the tray. "I didn't get us any cakes... it totally slipped my mind." He nudged Lisa on her arm with his elbow. "See, it's not just you that's forgetful. I don't have an excuse though. I was standing right there and staring at all those goodies while I was waiting in the queue."

"Oh, don't worry about it. It's a little too early in the day and I probably shouldn't anyway." Lisa felt self-conscious about the weight she had gained since giving birth. "Peter can be a fussy little bugger when it comes to what he eats and drinks," she said, before she took another sip of her drink. She noticed that Bill had a small smear of lipstick across his cheek. *Should I point it out to him? No, I think I'll let him explain that one to his wife.*

The weather took an unexpected turn for the worse as the skies appeared to darken. Lisa and Bill looked over at the hail stones that were thrashing against the window. "Looks like we could get some snow," Bill said, before he changed the subject. "Anyway, how long is it since we last saw each other?" He tipped his cup to his lips, blew away some of the steam and slurped on his drink. Peering over the rim at her, he waited for a response.

Rumbles of thunder grew louder as the door to the café opened. Lisa and Bill both turned their heads and watched as an elderly gentleman with noticeable white hair walked in. He was a priest and was dressed all in black, apart from his white clerical collar. Everyone looked, but no one wanted to be the one to ask him to move away from the door. It remained open and the cold air rushed in. He looked over at Lisa before he stared out through the window.

Lisa continued to watch the priest. She felt that she should know him. "Not sure exactly," she responded, before turning back to look at Bill. *This coffee tastes good, but then it always does when someone else makes it for you.* "I'd say it's been a good few years. Which is strange because I wonder why we haven't bumped into each other before. It's only a small town, after all." Bill began fidgeting on his seat as though he was finding it difficult to get comfortable. *Is now the right time to ask him about Susan? But, he's not answerable to me. It's got nothing to do with me. We're old news.*

"You know me, I've been busy working and... well, looking after Gillian." Bill gauged Lisa's response before he continued and decided that he should change the subject. "Anyway, are you still working at that bed and breakfast place?"

The café got brighter as lightning illuminated the sky. It lasted for several seconds. The road outside emptied as people took shelter wherever they could. Peter stirred to put his head to the other side of the pushchair.

"Sure am, I've been there for a good few years now." Lisa began counting on her fingers, underneath the table, as she tried to work out how long she had worked there. *Should I tell him that I'm leaving my job and moving away? Would he really give a damn if I did?*

Bill made an announcement and made that decision easier for Lisa. "I always wanted children of my own, but I guess it was never meant to be."

"What do you mean? Why wasn't it meant to be?" Lisa could not help but look surprised. She did not give him the chance to answer and continued, "Is it because Gillian's disabled?"

"Oh no, to the contrary. Gillian was capable of having children. In fact, she wanted them as much as me. I was the one that let the team down. Well me and my little swimmers," Bill said. *Does she really want to hear all this?* "My sperm count is so low that it doesn't take much effort to count them and no doubt, by now, every last one of them would fail to get a swimming certificate."

"I'm sorry to hear that. I had no idea." Lisa placed her hand over the top of Bill's. *Why did he never mention this to me before? He's got to be mistaken. He should have got a second opinion. A few of them had to have been Olympic champions or how is Peter here? Hang on… is this another one of his lies?*

"We both got tested a number of years ago and presumed that it would be Gillian that would be the one to have fertility problems, but I guess it serves me right really." Bill appeared to be so matter-of-fact. "After what I did to Gillian, Karma decided to come along and bite me on my arse. Although, it's always seemed unfair as it feels like she's being punished twice for wanting to be with me."

He's pretty convincing. I'll give him that. Isn't he going to put his extra marital affairs into that equation as well? Why didn't I see it sooner? My son's father is an absolute dickhead. The heavens rumbled as lightning struck the television aerial on the roof of the building on the opposite side of the road. Lisa looked towards the door. It was closed and the priest had gone. *It seems that I don't actually know anything about Bill. He always was the secretive one. He and Susan are probably better* matched. *They're both devious cunts.* "How is your wife?" she asked, as she turned to look at him.

"Yes, Gillian's doing okay. That's kind of you to ask." Bill smiled. He had not noticed the sarcasm in Lisa's voice. "Anyway, do I know the father?" He nodded towards Peter.

Shall I make up a name and make out that Peter was conceived from a one-night stand? That would surprise him. No... that's a stupid idea. He'll never believe me. What am I supposed to say? Should I change the subject and ask him about Susan?

"Hey, Lisa, it's okay. You don't have to tell me you know. Not if you don't want to. I didn't mean to sound so nosey." Bill tilted his head to one side and wondered if she might still want to answer his question. "Well, all I can say is that he's one hell of a lucky guy to have the two of you."

Lisa's coffee had cooled. Picking up her cup, she took a mouthful and looked around the café. *Please let me see someone who looks vaguely familiar. I need some sort of a distraction.* She felt awkward. She had made her decision. *I'm not going to tell him that he's Peter's father and I'm not going to make up a story.* "I'm not with Peter's father or with anyone else." She hoped that would put an end to the matter.

Looking at Peter, Lisa thought that his timing was perfect. He was awake and sitting, wide-eyed as he watched Bill with an apparent interest. His stare was not as intense as before, but it remained constant. Lisa noted

83

Peter's unusual behaviour, but Bill did not appear to have noticed. Nothing could have been further from the truth as he tried not to make eye contact with him.

Lisa could feel the awkward atmosphere. "I think he likes you," she said as she tried to lighten the mood. "Well something about you certainly seems to be grabbing his attention."

"You don't say." Bill could not stop himself from looking at Peter as a magnetic energy appeared to pull him in.

Peter chuckled. He liked playing that game with Bill. It was fun.

Bill scowled. He wanted Peter to stop looking at him as it was making him feel ill. *Why isn't Lisa telling him to stop whatever it is that he's doing?* He started to feel dizzy and like he might vomit. *Take deep breaths. This is all just in your imagination. For goodness sake, pull yourself together. He's just a little boy. What harm could such a small person possibly do?*

Lisa was out of her seat and standing next to Peter. Detecting that Bill was irritated, she tried to divert Peter's attention. She leant forward and brushed his fringe to one side with her fingertips. That didn't work. Leaning down further, her head was blocking his line of sight. That worked. Peter moved his eyes to watch Lisa pick up the cover from the floor. She folded it, placed it over the back of the pushchair and tucked it behind his head. "Do you want some juice, or would you prefer milk, Peter?"

"Milk," Peter stated.

"And what's the magic word, Peter?" Lisa raised her eyebrows and gave him that look that most mothers use on their child as she waited for him to use his manners.

Peter repeated himself and emphasised his forgotten word, "Milk, please."

Lisa messed up Peter's hair with the palm of her hand. "Good lad." She felt proud as she reached to get her bag from the floor. Placing it onto her chair, she unzipped it and searched inside. *Where's my damn purse hiding?* Bill pulled out his wallet and took out a ten-pound note. He held out his hand and waited until Lisa had taken the money from him. "Thanks, I'll empty my bag out and have another look when I've got Peter's drink. I know my purse is in here somewhere. I've only just used it in the shop."

"Hey, stop stressing. It doesn't matter. I said that it was going to be my treat."

Walking towards the counter, Lisa turned her head to look at Bill. Peter saw the glint in her eye and was not impressed. Who did this man think he was, appearing from nowhere and making his mother act different? He did not like him and did not want him hanging around. *This man's got to go.*

Bill stopped looking at Lisa and turned his gaze to the floor. He was aware that Peter was watching him with a look that felt like it was burning into his soul. Peter began lowering his head and to the point where you could not see him doing it, but his stare continued. Bill reached out and put his hand onto one of Peter's knees. He believed that he knew the reason for his hostile behaviour. "It's okay. I know that you're feeling jealous, but I promise you, hand on heart, that I'm not here to take your mummy away from you. We're just friends and I hope..." Bill was interrupted by Peter kicking out his leg. It made contact with his arm.

"Shut up and get off me," Peter murmured.

Liberating Peter from his touch, Bill got to his feet. He felt frustrated as he was not able to chastise him. He wanted to shout at him and slap his legs, but he thought better of it. Releasing the brake on the pushchair, he manoeuvred it so that Peter was not able to stare at him. He put the brake back on.

The hailstones had stopped and turned to light rain.

The queue had lengthened at the counter. Lisa was located to the middle. She was chatting to the lady that was standing behind her. Bill and Peter sat in silence. The two of them had chosen to ignore each other as they waited for her to return. Looking into his cup, Bill drank the last few drops of his coffee before he wiped around his mouth. He noted that Lisa had drunk half of hers and no doubt the remainder was at best, tepid and would be cold before she was able to finish it.

"Everything okay?" Lisa asked as she returned with Peter's milk carton in one hand and Bill's change in the other.

Bill shrugged. "Not sure."

"Thanks again." Lisa placed a five-pound note and some loose change onto the palm of Bill's hand. She noticed that Peter's pushchair had been moved. "What's happened?" She punctured the straw into the milk carton and, with care, passed it to Peter. With little effort, he put his hands up to take his drink from her. His eyes were filled with tears and his bottom lip was sticking out.

"A tantrum." Bill placed the note inside his wallet.

"You've moved his pushchair." Lisa picked up her bag from the chair and placed it onto the floor.

Bill was not sure if Lisa was asking him a question or making a statement. "Yes, I have," he responded. His tone was firm. He had decided that it was best to get the situation sorted.

"Why?" Lisa sniggered. "Surely it's not because he was staring at you?"

Bill did not appreciate being mocked. He counted to ten, in his head, before he answered, "Well yes, actually. You do realise that staring at people is not normal behaviour. I've just tried to explain how things are between you and me and he just kicked out."

"He's just a child for goodness sake." Lisa looked bewildered. "What is it that you were trying to explain to him exactly?"

Peter twisted himself and peered around the edge of his pushchair. He was watching Bill. Though Bill was not able to see Peter's mouth, he knew that he was smiling and trying to taunt him. "Yes, I do realise that he's only a child." Bill quietened his voice. He did not want to argue with Lisa. "I believe that he's acting up because he thinks that I'm going to come between the two of you. I tried to tell him that you and I are just friends." He paused to take a breath before he continued, "Lisa, please listen to me. You can't just let him sit there and stare at people or allow him to lash out."

The storm had passed, and the sun was attempting to burn through the clouds.

Grabbing her coat from the seat, Lisa put it on. She picked up her bag and hung its strap over her shoulder before she grabbed the packet of toilet rolls and placed them on Peter's knee. Looking at Bill, she said, "Thanks for the drinks, but it's time that we were going. It's been really nice to see you again and have a catch up. You take good care of yourself." She appeared void of emotion.

Bill had not expected that response. "Yes, I will." He knew that he should have jumped up and tried to stop Lisa from leaving, but he remained seated and watched as she pushed Peter's pushchair through the clutter of tables and chairs.

Lisa attempted to grab the door handle but could not reach it. A young man, who was standing outside, had noticed her struggle and pulled on the door handle, holding the door open for her. He saw her tears as he waited for her to leave. Keeping her head down, she thanked him.

The truth was that Bill was powerless to do anything. An invisible force was holding him down. He could not move from his chair and his drowsiness was rendering his ability to speak. *I'm sure that Lisa knows about Susan. She seemed so cold towards me. I need to explain that Susan was just a bit of fun. She means... meant nothing to me. It was her that approached me. She's the one that's been doing all the running and won't leave me alone.*

It wasn't until Lisa and Peter were out of sight that Bill was able to move. Ordering himself another coffee from the counter, he would wait in case Lisa returned.

Chapter Six
Afterlife

Fred had decided to go for a stroll. It was late, but the fresh air would clear his mind. The shop door opened as he walked towards it. Its bell was silent. He stepped outside. The door closed itself behind him. *There's snow on the ground. When did that happen? Strange, it doesn't feel cold enough for it to snow.* Drawing in long deep breaths, he could feel the exaggerated movements of his chest as it lowered and rose.

Glancing through each shop window as he passed them, Fred could see no sign of life. It was usual for someone to be sorting things out, like cleaning, tidying, stock taking or cashing up. Every restaurant and public house was in darkness. The clear night sky was bare of the moon and stars with a blackness that was as dark as ebony. There were no sounds of drunken behaviour or merriment as a stillness prevailed while the folk of the village slept.

I wonder what the time is. Fred looked over at the church clock to check. Its face was illuminated, but he could not make out the time. The clock's face was hazy, as though someone had drawn it in pencil and tried to smudge it away with their fingertip.

Feeling a desire to walk in the direction of Beechwood Park, Fred stood on the edge of the kerb and checked both ways of the deserted road. While crossing, he started to sing The Green Cross Code song, but he froze to the spot when he was dazzled by oncoming headlights. The vehicle was several feet away. Without making a sound, it had appeared from nowhere. Its brakes screeched as it tried to come to a stop. He shielded his eyes with the backs of his hands, held his breath and waited for the inevitable impact.

A few seconds went by. Fred was standing in the middle of the road. He was aware that he had not felt any impact as he moved his hands away from his eyes. There was no sign of a vehicle of any description, but in its place were two elderly ladies crossing the road in the opposite direction. He thought they looked familiar.

Fred made it to the other side of the road and leant against the stone wall of the bridge. He turned to watch as the ladies continued to dawdle as they crossed. *Now, where have I seen those two ladies before? Are they going to a fancy-dress party? Aren't they a little too old for that sort of thing?* Both of them were dressed in old fashioned attire and they were without colour.

The ladies seemed unaware that Fred was standing there as they chatted about their plans for that weekend. Their voices drifted as though he were walking alongside them. The tall slim lady was helping with the flowers for a wedding in the church that Saturday and the short rotund lady was going to have her hair done by her best friend's daughter. He was not able to hear the end of their conversation but carried on watching them as they walked past his shop and until they were out of sight, around the bend of the road.

I'm just having one of them vivid dreams. I'll wake up soon to the tunes on my clock radio. Fred suddenly remembered where he had seen those two ladies before. *They're on one of the framed photographs in the pool room of The Royal Oak. The one that's dated 1899.*

Following them, Fred walked along the path until he was standing where the two ladies had crossed. He checked both ways before he crossed the road, but he did not sing this time. Walking past his shop, he made his way to the corner, where he had lost sight of them, and looked up that road. They were nowhere to be seen. It was a long straight uphill route with no houses or passageways leading from it. *It's just not possible. They can't have reached the top. They were walking too slowly. Where did they go?* He shook his head, turned around and found himself wandering towards the park again.

En-route, Fred stopped and leant over the bridge. He looked down into the river that flowed beneath. Its waters were clearer than usual for the time of year.

The sound of a vehicle braking made Fred turn his head and witness the scene of those two ladies crossing the road in the same place and two bright lights, depicting headlights, could be seen. The two ladies failed to notice the brightness as it passed through them and faded to nothing.

A gurgling sound emanated from the river. Fred looked and witnessed a body floating towards him. It was Vicky's. Her once lengthy blonde hair had turned grey as it swirled around her head. Her thin body was deteriorating, and her face was unrecognisable, but he knew that it was her. *Come on, Fred, time to wake up before you give yourself a bloody heart-attack!*

Fred turned to look at the two ladies. They were walking past his shop and were about to go out of sight. A number of questions began racing through his mind. *If I'm not dreaming, then what the hell's going on? Why does everything appear so different, yet so familiar at the same time? And why do those two ladies from a nineteenth-century photograph appear to be on some kind of a time loop?*

Fred looked at the river and noticed that a square board was floating in the distance. It was making its way towards him. It was a Ouija board that was bobbing up and down on the water's surface and unbeknown to him, it was the same one that he had given away to a young man in his shop, many years earlier. The board passed under the bridge and out of sight.

Weeping could be heard as Vicky's body began drifting towards Fred; however, on this occasion something was holding her back. He was not able to see what was hindering her but could hear her screams.

Something looked different about Vicky as she got closer. Her face was distorted, as though her soul were tortured. *There's nothing that I can do.* Fred felt disorientated as he continued on his way. He listened to the distant sounds of the invisible vehicle slamming on its brakes and the pitiful noises of the young lady on the river.

An upstairs light came on in a room of a house across the road. Fred stopped and looked. He could make out a silhouette through the blind. Their arms were held out in front of them as they walked across the room before whoever it was switched off the light. *Could be a sleepwalker or even a zombie, especially with the day that I'm having?*

Street lamps flickered as the sound of electricity buzzed through the air. Black wispy shadows emerged beneath each light as far as the eye could see.

Snow began to fall. Fred had left the shop without putting on a coat. Stretching his arms out in the front of him, he looked up towards the heavens. He could not feel the sensation of the snow hitting him or the biting temperature of the night.

As though he were a young boy, an unexpected urge made Fred jump from the path and into the road. He reached and tried to grab a handful of snow to make a snowball, but he was not able to pick it up. He stood there for a moment longer before he turned to look at his footsteps and discovered that there were no imprints of where he had trodden. There was now a fresh blanket of snow laid over the village.

Chapter Seven
The Beechwood Country Manor Hotel

Lisa and Peter were uninvited guests at a wedding reception party that was taking place at The Beechwood Country Manor Hotel; a large hotel that was located to the outskirts of the village. Her apartment had sold and, as yet, she had not managed to find them a new home. She had put their furniture and personal possessions into a secure lock-up and for the foreseeable future they would live out of suitcases while they stayed at the hotel.

The bride looked stunning in her long white gown; although, she was a little worse for wear as she tried to maintain her balance, along with her dignity, while she danced around the edge of the dance floor. Some type of magnetic force field appeared to prevent her from stumbling beyond its boundary. It was not a private event and some of the other hotel residents had gate-crashed the occasion. The invited guests would, from time to time, guide the bride back to the centre of the dance floor and ensure that she had no humiliating collisions with the surrounding furniture or worse, she came face to face with the floor.

The groom had removed his jacket and tie and was propped against the bar. He had unfastened the top two buttons of his shirt which revealed several long chest hairs trying to make a bid for freedom. It was possible that he was the happiest man on the planet. He appeared to have drunk his own body weight in alcohol and the odds were stacked against him being able to perform his wedding night obligations. His feet tapped, though not in time to the music, and he sang lyrics to a different song than the one that was being played by the flamboyant disc jockey. Guests were partying like they were not expecting to go out for the rest of the year. The bar staff were kept busy and as the night progressed, the music got louder as did some of the guests.

Peter was dancing in the corner of the room, to the side of where Lisa was seated. He threw out his arms and legs, in an ill-timed manner, and yet, he appeared to be more in time to the music than either the bride or groom, but he could be forgiven for his lack of rhythm as he was only a child.

Tiredness caught up with Peter and made him lose his balance. As he fell, he burst into tears before he had even touched the floor. He curled up on his side, put his thumb into his mouth and began sucking on it while his index finger rubbed the end of his nose. He tried, in vain, to fight his tiredness, but his eyes closed, and he dropped off into a deep sleep. The sounds of the music, chatter and laughter failed to waken him.

A pregnant woman, who was in her last trimester, and her partner were sitting at the next table. She was watching Peter with interest and appeared to have a permanent smile etched across her face. Nudging her partner, with her elbow, she pointed at Peter and said, "Aw, look at him." She turned her head to check that her partner was looking.

Lisa noticed that there were two cans of diet coke on the couples table. *Poor fella, he looks like he needs a proper drink inside him. He's probably not allowed any because she's not drinking.* She picked Peter up and lifted him with care, as she did not want to waken him. Looking over at the couple, she said, "He's tired himself out with all that spinning around and dancing."

The couple did not hear Lisa, but they both smiled and nodded their heads.

As she sat, Lisa cradled Peter against her arm. She stroked his fringe away from his eyes and looked at him. *He looks so much like his grandfather. Even more so, the older he gets and especially when he's sleeping.* She would often look at the photograph of her father which she carried around in her purse. "I think it's time that I drank up and got this little one up to his bed." She had started to feel uncomfortable with the brooding woman's staring. Putting her glass to her lips, she drank the rest of her gin and tonic in one mouthful and followed it with an overstated gulp and a stifled belch. She shuffled forward on her seat and managed to stand up without disturbing Peter.

Peter felt heavy as Lisa carried him along the corridor with his head resting on her shoulder. She stepped inside the lift, pressed the button for the third floor and watched as the door closed. *I'm really in the mood for another drink, but it's probably a good thing that Peter's fallen asleep as it'll save me the pain of a hangover in the morning.*

The key card to the hotel room door worked, flashing blue, on Lisa's first try. It had been known to take her several attempts.

She looked at the alarm clock. Its digital numbers stood out in the darkened room. It read ten thirty. *Wow, it feels much earlier than that. I hadn't realised what the time was. I've obviously been down at the bar for longer than I thought. How much alcohol have I actually drunk? Who knows? Who cares? It's doubtful that anyone else was taking the time to count. Anyway, I feel sober, so does it really matter? It's not as though I've got some kind of special relationship with alcohol. I just have the occasional tipple when the mood takes me.*

Lisa put Peter on top of his duvet. He turned onto his side and curled up into the foetal position. Leaving his clothes on, she unfastened the laces on his shoes. One was knotted, as usual. She slipped his shoes and socks off and put them down at the side of his bed before she double checked on the time. *It's no wonder that Peter's so tired. It's way past his bedtime.*

With her make-up removed and teeth brushed, Lisa turned off the light in the en-suite bathroom. The bedroom was in darkness except for the light from the corridor which seeped in through the gaps to each side of the door. She noticed that the door was ajar. She was certain that she had closed it. Opening it, with caution, she checked outside. Several people were congregated outside the lift and were talking. They stopped mid-conversation and turned to look at her. She shuddered as a bitter coldness passed through her and every hair on her body appeared to stand on end. She looked over at Peter. He was in the same position, undisturbed. She closed the door and it clicked shut. She pulled the chain across.

Lisa climbed into her bed and pulled the duvet over her shoulder. Its cover felt cold with a crisp starchiness and despite the beds being changed that morning the bedding did not smell fresh. Her eyelids soon became heavy and she drifted off into a sleep.

It felt like only seconds later when, in a drowsy state, Lisa was awoken by the guests who were staying in the next room. Their door, slamming shut, had startled her as they returned from their night of drunken merriment. Other doors along the corridor began to close.

Peter did not stir. Lisa could hear him snoring. His night terrors appeared to be behind him.

Ignoring her neighbours, Lisa turned over and tried to get back to sleep, but loud voices could be heard in the corridor outside the neighbouring room. The younger guests had assembled there before they knocked on the door. Every sound appeared to echo along the corridor. It would appear that the downstairs wedding party was to continue next door, of all the rooms in the hotel.

Remaining still, Lisa listened to drinking glasses as they clanged together and to a party game of throwing empty beer cans, over and over again, into a metal wastepaper bin. Her neighbour's voices got louder, and the sound of one woman's laughter stood out from the others. She appeared to find everything, that was said or done, hysterical. Other guests arrived and knocked on the door and with each new caller came a round of applause. The time was one a.m. and the celebrations were well under way.

Peter began to stir. His toenails scraped along his cover as he wriggled and groaned with an obvious annoyance at the commotion. Lisa leapt out of bed. Her patience was starting to dwindle. She stopped herself from hitting the connecting wall and went to sit on the edge of Peter's bed. She stroked his face with the backs of her fingers as she tried to calm him. His skin felt hot and sticky to the touch. She needed to cool him. Pulling the curtain along, she opened one of the large sash windows a couple of inches. Cool air rushed in. The light from an outside lamp shone through. He soon settled, closed his eyes and dozed off.

Lisa noticed that the room next door was quieter, but she could feel someone watching her. She looked over at the door. There appeared to be a silhouette, but she could not make out who it was. She shuffled forward to get a better look. *Who the hell is it and what are they doing in my room?* "Hello," she called out.

But whoever it was, they did not respond.

Moving forward, Lisa squinted as she tried to get a better look at who it might be. *How long have they been in the room with us? Have they been watching us while we've been sleeping? Is it a pervert?* The figure remained still as though they were there to observe. As she got closer, she recognised him. It was that priest from the café. He turned around and walked through the closed door.

Standing there for a moment longer, Lisa stared at the door. She was waiting to see if the priest was going to reappear. *Who is he exactly and what does he want? Why's he following us?*

When Lisa was satisfied that there would be no return visit from the priest that night, she got into bed and pulled up the duvet. Closing her eyes, she tossed and turned while attempting to get to sleep.

Drifting, the same dream started where the last one had finished, but no sooner had Lisa started to feel herself relax and fall into that vision, when she was disturbed. This time it was the sound of footsteps stampeding against the floor. Without thinking, she leapt out of bed and smacked the wall with the palm of her hand several times. Her hand began smarting. She grimaced as she rubbed it.

However, on this occasion, Lisa was mistaken as those particular noises had not come from the next room. A game of chase was being played along the corridor and the footsteps sounded like they belonged to small children. Her suspicions were confirmed when she heard young girls giggling outside the door. Rubbing her sore palm, she tiptoed to look through the spyhole. She was able to hear their footsteps but could see nothing other than the doors on the opposite side of the corridor. A chilling draught blew under the gap of the door and over her bare feet.

The stillness from the next room was short-lived as their volume rose with the sounds of loud chatter and embellished laughter. Lisa was worn out from all the disturbances and could not stop herself from clenching her right hand and thumping the wall with the side of her fist. A sharp pain shot up from her little finger to her elbow. The wall shook. A framed watercolour of a scenic landscape fell from a small supporting nail and the glass within its frame smashed on impact with the bedside cabinet.

Peter sat upright and rubbed his eyes. He was tired and disorientated as he looked around the room. "Mummy?"

"It's okay, sweetheart." Lisa walked over to comfort Peter. Picking him up, she hugged him and patted his back with a gentle rhythm as though mimicking a heartbeat. She whispered into his ear, "I'm sorry for waking you. It's just me being silly and getting cross. I just lost it for a second because there are some really thoughtless people in this hotel." He rested his head against her shoulder, put his thumb into his mouth and started to fall asleep.

A number of the guests could be heard leaving the room next door. They were inebriated and struggling to put their slurred words in the right order to make coherent sentences. Staggering along the corridor, they bumped into walls, each other, guest's doors and the wall-mounted fire extinguishers.

Lisa put Peter on his bed. He stirred to pull his duvet over him, turned and laid in his favourite position as though by second nature. His skin temperature had cooled. She closed the window and, with both hands, held it so that it did not drop, and slam shut. Opening the curtains further, she needed to be able to see where the broken glass had fallen without needing to switch on a light. As she felt the smoothness of the curtains velvet fabric, she found herself stroking it. She stood there for a moment longer and looked beyond her reflection and into the night.

Lisa made her way towards her bed. The glass from the picture frame had broken into four triangular pieces, which were almost identical in size. She picked up the frame and put it onto the bedside cabinet. So as not to cut her fingers, she picked up each piece of glass with care. Placing them inside the frame, she propped it against the wastepaper bin. *Not sure how I'm going to explain that one to that lovely lady from housekeeping tomorrow.*

The party in the next room was in full swing with an accompaniment of revellers along the corridor. Lisa laid on her bed and tried to focus on Peters breathing. *At least he's managing to sleep through it. Just don't go and disturb him, again, Lisa.* She pushed the duvet from her legs and sat up.

The floorboards creaked as Lisa tiptoed towards the door. She looked through the spyhole and saw that one of the bridesmaids, from the reception party, and two young men were walking up and down the full length of the corridor. The three of them were sniggering, like small children, while they tried to walk in a straight line. She looked at the alarm clock. *Bloody hell, its two thirty in the morning.*

Grabbing her mobile telephone from the dressing table, Lisa turned on its torch and pointed it at the numbers on the landline telephone. She picked up the handset and pressed 'zero' for reception. It continued to ring out before she ascertained that no one was going to pick it up at the other end. *Strange, I thought it was supposed to be a twenty-four-hour manned service and it's unlikely that someone's checking in at this time of night.*

Lisa dialled 'one'. This number was supposed to be for the night porter, but she had no success. *Isn't the clue supposed to be in the job title? Maybe they're all having their own party or just catching up on a bit of sleep.* She put the handset down, picked it up again and then dialled the same number. Still there was no answer. *Maybe all the extension numbers just go through to the same person.*

Taking an audible breath, Lisa dialled 'four' for room service. *If no one bothers to answer this time, then I'll walk down every corridor of this hotel, in my nightwear, until I find a member of staff that will make those damn guests shut the fuck up.* The telephone rang once before a polite young man answered, "Room service, how can I help you?"

"Hi, it's room twenty-seven. I'm sorry to bother you, but there's an awful lot of noise coming from the room next door to us. We're trying to sleep, but it's just impossible. Do you think that you might be able to have a word with them?"

"When you say noise, what do you mean exactly?"

Lisa took the handset away from her ear and glared at it. *I'm tired and really not in the fucking mood for this idiot's stupidity. What does it matter what type of noise?* But she remained composed and said, "Excessively loud laughter, you know, general antisocial behaviour. They're having a party and it's really not acceptable, especially when it's two thirty in the morning. It's been going on for hours now and like I said, my son and I are trying to sleep."

"I don't think that there have been any other complaints from any of the other neighbouring rooms."

105

"Well, there wouldn't have been, would there?" Lisa said, and because of the room service man's flippancy, her composure was gone, "All the other neighbouring rooms are next door in that same fucking party."

"I'll send someone up and ask them to quieten things down. I'm sorry for any inconvenience that's been caused."

"Thank you," Lisa said. *Now that wasn't hard, was it?* She placed the handset onto its cradle, walked over to the door and waited.

The room service man was true to his word. Within a couple of minutes, he had managed to track down the night porter. He walked past Lisa's bedroom door, as she looked through the spyhole, and knocked on the door of the next room. A number of guests could be heard volunteering to answer.

Lisa glanced over at Peter. He was sleeping. *How's that even possible with all this racket that's going on around us?* She pressed her ear against the door, so that she was able to hear what the night porter was saying.

"Good evening, folks... or should I say, morning? I hope that you're all enjoying your stay with us at The Beechwood Country Manor Hotel. I'm terribly sorry to bother you while you're all obviously having so much fun, but we have had a complaint from room twenty-seven about the excessive noise that's coming from this room." The night porter paused for a moment and let out a deep exaggerated breath, as though expressing that he did not want to be a killjoy and that he was just doing his job. "If I could ask you all kindly to keep the noise down and then hopefully, we can keep everyone happy."

Sporadic apologies, in the forms of overstated shouting and slurred words, could be heard as some of them started to disband onto the corridor. They would find their way to their rooms after pointless conversations, some of which took place outside Lisa's door.

The bridesmaid and her two devoted male companions reappeared after laying low. Taking it in turns, the three of them continued to play 'who can walk in a straight line without falling over'. They chatted and talked over each other, about any subject that popped into their heads before they laughed and attempted to knock each other onto the floor. This behaviour would continue until five thirty.

Lisa had resigned herself to the fact that she would not be getting any sleep that night. She slouched in the rooms only chair, propped her feet on her bed and looked through the opening of the curtains. The sheep in the nearby fields would start with their bleating in an hour or two. In the night sky, a black cloud loomed on the horizon.

The hotel was quiet, as the partygoers would, no doubt, be asleep in their beds; however, the other guests would be starting to wake and go about their business and the whole door slamming scenario would start over.

Lisa had failed to notice that Peter was awake and sitting with his eyes wide open. He was staring beyond her and towards the area of the door. Something had caught his attention and was amusing him. It was the sound of his giggling that made her turn her head to see what was entertaining him, but all she could see was their suitcases, coats and shoes. There did not appear to be anything interesting or the slightest bit funny. She saw that he was pointing towards the doorway. "There's a girl," he said, as his eyes lit up at the thought of a new friend wanting to play. He began to wave. "Look, Mummy, she's sticking her tongue out."

I can't see anyone. Lisa thought, peering in the same direction, to no avail. She got up from the chair, walked over to Peter and sat to the side of him. *Perhaps if I tried to look at her from a different angle that might help.* It did. *Yes… there she is.* He began jumping up and down, like he was on a spring, as he continued to point at the door. "Don't you see her?"

"Yes, darling." Lisa brushed her hand through Peter's hair as she tried to calm him. The hairs on the back of her neck stood on end. *My god, that ghost girl looks like she's been here since the hotel was built.* The temperature in the room plummeted, but she ignored all the signs of the presence that was in the room with them. "Why are you laughing, you cheeky monkey?"

"Can I play with her?" Peter looked at Lisa with pleading eyes. "Please," he added as an afterthought and because he hoped that using his manners would help him in his plight.

How am I supposed to explain to Peter that there isn't really a little girl there for him to play with? Lisa looked at the ghost, who was waiting to see what the answer would be. But she avoided the issue and said the first thing that came into her head, "Not at the moment. It's a little bit too early for all that running around." She walked over to the dressing table and switched on its light. A soft radiance lit part of the room.

Despite the girl fading, Peter continued to look at the doorway. His bottom lip was sticking out and his eyes were filling with tears. Lisa felt a tinge of guilt as she sat beside him. She put her hand underneath his chin and lifted his face so that she could see his expression. "Whatever's the matter?"

Peter did not answer.

He's probably just sleepy. But, how am I supposed to explain to him that it's okay for him to play with a ghost? She wiped her thumb to the underside of Peter's eyes to remove his tears and hugged him. *It looks like I'll need to have that chat with him about the supernatural, sooner rather than later. I'll need to explain that a lot of grown-ups pretend that there's no such thing, even though they've witnessed unexplainable phenomenon themselves and some, on more than one occasion.*

Someone in the neighbouring room, to the opposite side of where the party had taken place, let out a loud fart. Lisa raised her eyebrows in surprise, smiled and looked at Peter. The two of them laughed.

Peter laid on his bed, put his thumb into his mouth and closed his eyes. Lisa pulled the duvet over him. Balancing herself on the edge of his bed, she laid to the side of him and the two of them drifted off into a peaceful sleep.

A couple of hours had passed when Lisa awoke to the sound of Peter giggling. He was standing to the side of her and poking his little finger up her left nostril. She moved her head so that he could not reach.

Manoeuvring her body was proving to be difficult, as Lisa had laid in the same position for the duration of her nap. After losing all sensation in her right arm, she rolled onto her stomach and waited for the hot tingling sensations to stop, as blood flowed through her veins.

Lisa rubbed her arm with vigour, as she stood by the window and looked at the rolling hillsides. The sheep in the neighbouring fields had flocked together by the dry-stone walls to gain shelter from the imminent wet weather.

Peter was quiet. Lisa turned around and discovered that his mischievous mood was to continue. He was looking into the dressing table mirror and pouting while applying one of her lipsticks. It was a ruby red one and most of it had not made contact with his lips. She took the lipstick from him. Reaching for her make-up remover and cotton wool, she said, "You're a little bit too young yet, Peter, to be borrowing Mummy's make-up. By the look of it, I think that you will probably need a little bit more practice before you go outside with it on."

Peter's sniggering soon stopped when Lisa began wiping the lipstick off his face. His wriggling was making it difficult, but she managed to hold his head still. Despite her best efforts, the skin around his mouth remained pink.

Cramming the lipstick and other make-up into her bulging cosmetics bag, Lisa forced the zip to close and hid the bag away, out of Peter's reach. She glanced at herself in the mirror and imagined the worst possible reflection would look back at her, but her attention was drawn to the framed picture, which she had placed next to the bin. It was hanging above her bed. She turned to double check and there it was. "Peter, have you picked anything up from the side of the bin?" *That's unlikely, Lisa. He wouldn't even be able to reach up there to rehang it.*

Peter was laying on his belly on the duvet of his bed. He had retrieved a number of small action figures from the windowsill and was playing with them with the usual accompaniment of sound effects. He stopped for a moment and scowled in Lisa's direction. He was hesitant to answer as he thought he had misheard her. "No."

Standing to the side of her bed, Lisa looked at the picture to examine it. The cracks along the glass were visible, but she could only see them because she knew that they were there. *Who, why and when did someone fix it?* She stood for a moment longer and shook her head.

Placing the 'do not disturb' sign on the outside of the door, Lisa turned to Peter and said, "Right, little man, let's run a bath for you."

Peter did not need to be told twice. He climbed off his bed and ran towards the bathroom. His bare feet thudded small steps against the floor. "Let me do the bubbles... please," Peter begged as he tried to push Lisa to one side. He grabbed his bubble bath from the side of the bathtub with both hands gripped around it. It was a plastic bottle in the guise of a pirate, which was the main reason for him enjoying his bath times.

Lisa lifted Peter and moved him to one side so that she was able to reach the baths mixer tap. The right water temperature was flowing. She stood back and propped herself against the bathroom door frame.

With the lid of the bubble bath bottle removed, Peter stretched and poured more than was needed beneath the flow of the water.

"Now, don't go putting too much bubble bath in the water, Peter, or you'll fill the room with bubbles." Lisa smiled as he put the bottle with a wonky fitted lid on the side. "And be careful that you don't get any soap in your eyes today. Remember, it stings."

Peter got undressed. His top, trousers and underpants were all inside out and laying in different places on the tiled floor.

Lisa turned off the tap and because Peter did not like his baths hot, there was only a small amount of steam in the air. He climbed in. His face was just visible above the miniature mountain range of bubbles.

Although Lisa was sleepy, she felt content as she watched Peter whilst he played. "Shall we go down to the restaurant this morning and grab some breakfast? I think we deserve something special today. What do you think, Peter?"

"Beans on toast. Then I can do poopy noises." Peter gave Lisa one of his cheeky grins before he stuck out his tongue between his moistened lips and blew a raspberry. Fine droplets sprayed out from his mouth and each one landed on top of its own bubble before causing them to burst.

Lisa smiled. "After you've finished playing with those bubbles, don't forget that you need to clean those teeth." She pointed at his mouth.

Peter muttered something under his breath, but it was inaudible. Lisa presumed that he was in agreement and did not ask him to repeat himself. She brushed her teeth while she waited for him to finish bathing.

Peter began to giggle.

Lisa spat into the washbasin. She had toothpaste smeared around her mouth when she turned to see what was amusing Peter. A chill presented itself as he looked towards the doorway and his chuckling had been replaced with a serious expression. She rinsed her toothbrush under the cold running water and placed it into the tumbler that was on the shelf above the basin. The tap continued to run. Wiping away any residual toothpaste, she rinsed water over her face and dried herself on a hand towel. She turned and said, "It's time to pull the plug, Peter."

As usual, Peter stalled for time and pretended that he could not find the plug chain. Lisa moved towards the bath and he managed to locate it before she put her hand into his bath water. He pulled on the chain and wound it around the tap several times. They both listened to the water gurgle as it escaped down the plughole.

The chill was gone, and Peter said nothing about what he had seen. He sat and waited until the last trickle had seeped away. Covered in bubbles, he climbed out of the bath and shivered. His body was rigid as he dripped onto the bath mat. Lisa bundled him up in a bath towel and wrapped her arms around him. She carried him into the bedroom and put him on top of his bed. "Right, Peter, get yourself dried and dressed. Then get yourself back into that bathroom to brush them teeth."

After a tantrum about Peter not wanting to brush his teeth and an incident with an inside out, back to front, tee shirt, Lisa and Peter were ready to go for their breakfast.

A stale odour greeted them as they opened their room door. There was a small window at each end of the corridor, and they were never opened. Their room door slammed shut behind them and locked itself.

Making their way to the restaurant, Peter held Lisa's hand. His other arm was raised as he slid his hand along the rail while he descended the stairs. They walked past the desk in the foyer and the receptionist looked up to acknowledge them with a smile.

A poster that was on the noticeboard had grabbed Lisa's attention. A medium was going to be holding an event at the hotel that weekend. She was an American celebrity who had a television show, named Paranormal Pandora. She was able to communicate with the dead and convey messages back to the living. Lisa had seen her on some daytime television show and although not convinced, she would go along for the entertainment. Tickets were available from reception and were selling fast. However, before she bought a ticket, she would ask Elizabeth if she would like Peter to stay over with her for the weekend.

The restaurant doors were wedged open as Peter bolted through the opening. His head almost made contact with the corners of several tables as he swerved and ducked until he reached their usual table, which was next to the furthest window. Lisa shook her head. *It's only a matter of time before he knocks himself out. I've told him to slow down. But, will he listen?* It was the best positioned table in the restaurant, and their favourite, as the two of them could look into the garden and watch the birds feeding at the bird table.

Lisa was not in a hurry. She caught up to Peter and steadied the back of his chair as he climbed onto it. He made it look hard work. She pushed his chair closer to the table so that any dropped food or spillages would hit the table and not land on his lap. He placed his palms flat on the table and watched as she put the strap of her bag over the back of her chair. "Will you just watch my bag, Peter, while I go and get you your beans on toast?" His eyes widened as he stared at her bag. She noted his sarcasm.

Peter ate his breakfast, although there were more beans falling from his fork than going into his mouth. Lisa sat for a moment longer before she started to eat her croissant. *What can we do today? I know, after we've done some house hunting, I'll show Peter some more sights of Beechwood.*

Lisa and Peter watched a grey squirrel steal food from the bird table as they finished their breakfast.

Chapter Eight
The Wedding Party

The main road of Beechwood was blocked off to vehicles, as were the paths to all members of the public. Flashing blue lights of ambulances and police cars lit the air. Reporters with microphones leant over the police cordon tape as they tried to acquire information from any of the emergency services.

"Can you tell us what's happened?"

"How many people do you believe are involved?"

"Are there any fatalities amongst them?"

The police tried, in vain, to move people along as they continued to ignore the reporters.

Eager paramedics stood by their ambulances and waited for the fire crew to arrive.

Photographers were taking every opportunity to get that picture for the front page of their newspaper. They pushed and shoved to find a gap in the crowd for that perfect view. One of them climbed up the side of a lamp post after finding a window cleaners ladder left propped against a wall.

The local news crew was quick to arrive and set-up their equipment. A few people recognised the newsreader and were trying to get in on the shot. 'A major incident' is what the journalists were calling it.

It was almost lunchtime; Lisa and Peter had wanted to go to the chip shop for a bag of chips with bits, to share, but the two of them were standing and watching as the chaos unfolded in front of them.

The police had ordered the shopkeepers closest to the scene to close their premises. Their workers were escorted from the buildings to join the growing crowd of onlookers behind the tape. The tenants that lived in the flats above the shops watched with their noses flattened against their windows.

Lisa overheard part of a conversation between the two men that were standing to the side of her. "It sounds like there's been a serious coach accident. Someone said that they'd heard the driver was still pissed-up from last night. He went hurtling past them and nearly knocked them over."

A fire engine and two ambulances arrived behind them. The driver of the fire engine turned on the siren and gave a quick blast on his horn. Lisa grabbed Peter's hand, so that she did not lose him in the crowd of people that were rushing to get out of the way. A police officer removed the tape and the emergency vehicles that were already at the scene manoeuvred to allow them through. The tape was put back in place and everyone resumed their position.

The rain had stopped. Streams flowed alongside the kerbs as the water failed to find an escape route. The drains were blocked and filled with soil and debris which had set like concrete.

"I'm hungry," Peter said, as he rubbed his tummy and licked his lips.

"Come on, we'll go back to the hotel and get something to eat from there."

Lisa and Peter walked into the hotel foyer and found that it was busier than usual. It appeared that every member of staff was huddled behind the reception desk. Each of them looked serious as they stared at the television that was hanging from the wall in the corner of the room. The volume was loud as the subtitles flashed across the bottom of the screen. It was the local news and the reporters were talking about the accident in the village.

Lisa and Peter made their way into the restaurant. There wasn't anyone else in the room as they sat at their usual table and waited.

"A coach carrying what is believed to be a wedding party, has crashed in the village of Beechwood. It is not yet known how many people are involved. A number of eyewitnesses are reporting that the coach ploughed through the bridge and plunged into the river. The emergency services are at the scene. The main route is closed until further notice and there is a diversion in place...," the reporter said.

Peter looked out of the window as he swung his legs. Ten minutes had gone by and no one had come to take Lisa's order. *This is bloody ridiculous. I've waited long enough.* "Just stay here, Peter, I'll go find someone." She walked out of the restaurant and went up to the reception desk. No one had moved. They were all in the same positions. Not one of them looked at her. *Keep calm and do not shout or swear at them.* "Is it possible that someone can come and take my order? My little boy is starting to get hungry." She looked at each of them and wondered which one would respond.

"Yes, I'll be straight there," said one of the ladies. She followed Lisa through, with her notebook and pencil, and took her order. *See, that wasn't too difficult, was it? All that for a couple of plates of chips. Let's see how long it takes them to bring them over.* She watched as the waitress left. A couple walked into the restaurant and though they sat at a table at the other side of the room, she was still able to hear their conversation.

"I'm glad we decided to come in the car yesterday," said the lady. Her shoulders were slumped, and it sounded like she had been crying. "I know that sounds awful and I shouldn't even be thinking it, never mind saying it out loud."

"Don't worry about it. It's only what I was thinking. I'll tell you what, though. It's a bloody good job that you're pregnant and didn't want to travel on that coach or we would both have been in that accident," said the man. The couple looked down at their menus.

Lisa recognised that the man and pregnant lady were the same couple from the previous night's party.

Now it all makes sense. No wonder all the staff look so concerned.

The waitress brought over their chips. She feigned a smile.

"Thank you," Lisa and Peter said at the same time.

I bet them lot all think that I'm a right heartless cow and I care more about a plate of sodding chips than I do about that coach accident.

The pregnant lady looked over at Lisa and Peter and waved.

Peter did not notice.

Lisa smiled and nodded.

The bridesmaid and the driver had put their overnight bags in the luggage compartment and were standing outside, to the side of the coach door. They were hungover and did not care about the rain.

"You can't get behind that wheel. You're still well over the limit. If you get pulled over by the cops and breathalysed, then you're knackered," said Lily. As well as feeling nauseous, her head was pounding, and it got worse every time she moved. Her legs were aching from walking up and down the full length of the corridor for hours.

Jack unlocked the coach door and it swung open. "It's all well and good you saying that now, but if you remember, I wasn't supposed to be drinking at all. I asked you to get me a coke and what did you go and do?

You went and spiked it, you daft bint." He had not slept a wink and had spent the last hour drinking coffee.

An empty vodka bottle poked out of Lily's bag. She noticed it and chuckled. "Oh yeah, but we had fun, didn't we? I don't remember you complaining at the time."

Jack boarded the coach. "You're right though, if I do get caught or anything happens, then I'm going to get the sack." His hands were shaking. Turning around, he held them out to show Lily.

Looking at Jack, Lily noticed that his skin was a tinge of green, his lips were blue, and both of his eyes were bloodshot. "Just get one of the others to drive."

Jack scowled. "Who? Everyone's still pissed up and I very much doubt that anyone who's on this trip can drive a coach, do you?" He regretted shaking his head.

Sitting in the driver's seat, Jack reached over the steering wheel, picked up his sunglasses and put them on. He tried to act natural as his passengers boarded, well as normal as anybody that wears sunglasses on a cloudy morning can act. He started up the engine and turned on the air conditioning, but it did not appear to be working.

Lily sat on the seat behind Jack. The other guests, who had been present at that party which took place next door to Lisa's room, continued to board the coach. They were quiet as they found their seats. Some held up the queue as they put their bags in the overhead compartments. Seats were reclined. Jackets were rolled up, made into pillows and placed against the windows so they could rest their weary heads.

When it looked like everyone had boarded and got settled, Lily did a head count. Everyone appeared to be accounted for, well the number leaving on the coach was the same as what had arrived. "We're good to go, driver," she said to Jack, before she sat and rested her eyes.

Jack thought he was going to vomit. He got off the coach and left its engine running. Grabbing a bottle of water and a packet of aspirin from the side pocket of his rucksack, he placed two of the tablets on the back of his tongue, took a mouthful of water and gulped.

Opening her right eye, for a moment, Lily watched as Jack sat behind the steering wheel. He pressed a button for the door to close and put the coach into gear. It jerked forward before they were on their way.

Jack clipped the wing mirror of one of the upmarket cars in the hotels car park, but he could not afford to stop and report the damage. He carried on driving and pretended that he had not noticed. Some of the roads from the hotel were awkward where they narrowed in places, but he managed to get around them as they made their way towards the village of Beechwood.

Most of Jack's passengers were now sleeping, apart from the lady who had spent most of the previous hours laughing. She was occupying the coach's one toilet and filling it with the contents of her stomach. Nearby passengers began stirring when they smelt and heard her vomiting. They pulled out the paper sick bags that were provided on the rear of the seats in front of them. Some of them managed to spew into the bag whilst others got it on the floor or down the back of the seat that was in front of them.

Jack felt drowsy. He reached to slide the side window open, but it would not budge. *Damn, it's stuck. I'll have to get that fixed as well.* He had seen the farmer that was making his way along a side lane, in a tractor, and had expected him to stop when he reached the lane junction, but he pulled out, without bothering to look, right in front of the coach. Jack slammed on his brakes and yelled, "Fucking idiot!"

The farmer continued down the lane and, without turning around, he gave Jack the middle finger.

The coach jolted to a halt and the only seat belt that was fitted was for the driver. Lily woke as she flew forward and hit the back of Jack's seat. She put her hand to her nose, which had taken the brunt of the impact. It was bleeding and her vision was out of focus for a few moments before she lost consciousness.

A motorbike pulled up behind the coach, followed by two cars. One of the car drivers began tooting his car horn, then wound down his window and started shouting obscenities at Jack.

Jack lifted his foot from the brake pedal and the coach began edging forward. He was aware that Lily had hit the back of his seat and glanced sideways to check on her. "I'm so sorry, I can't pull up anywhere. I'll stop as soon as we get into the village. It should only be another minute or so."

Lily was not able to answer Jack. She was slumped behind his seat.

"Shit." Jack hit the steering wheel with the palm of his hand and shouted, "Is everyone else okay?" *You need to calm down or you're not going to get these folk to their destination*, he told himself.

There were several murmurs, but it was hard to determine if they were responses or strange noises from their hangovers and motion sickness.

The road widened. Jack looked into the right-hand wing mirror and saw that the motorbike was about to overtake him. He drove as close to the left as he could, so that the rider could get by, but as he passed Jack, he gave him the universal hand signal for 'wanker'. *Bloody charming.* He put up his hand, waved and shouted, "You're welcome."

Jack shuddered. He reached to try the air conditioning, but it was not budging. *Fucking hell, this coach is well and truly knackered! Doesn't anything work properly?* He could see the sign for Beechwood ahead. *I'll pull up near that bridge. I'll be blocking the road, but so what. The other drivers will just have to go around me, after all, this is a medical emergency.*

The aspirin had not kicked in. Jack's head was pounding, and he had started to sweat. He took his eyes off the road to rub them, but when he looked up there was someone or something in the road. It was a black shadow standing in front of the coach. He put his foot on the brake and swerved.

The coach screeched as it mounted the path, crashed through the bridge wall and plunged into the river below. Jack passed out, over the steering wheel, before the coach hit the water.

Chapter Nine
Melanie Willis

Lisa was taking Peter on another guided tour of Beechwood village, but to his dismay, this time the two of them were on foot. He was feeling lethargic and would have preferred the comfort of his pushchair or his mother's car. Anything that did not involve him having to put one foot in front of the other.

Walking up one of the villages steep roads, Peter found an excuse to stop every few steps. He crouched to pick up stones, small sticks and pieces of litter from the ground. He placed each item into one of his pockets. Stones and sticks went into one and all the rubbish went into another.

Lisa and Peter had managed to walk partway up a road when he stopped and refused to go any further. His legs had stopped working. She lifted him onto the nearest garden wall, so that he could sit for a while. Perching next to him, the two of them rested and looked across the valley.

It was not until Lisa turned her head and looked up that she realised where they were. The house looked smaller than what she remembered, and it appeared to be derelict. All the windows and curtains were closed.

The colours on the curtains had faded and the windows and front door were filthy with fumes from passing cars. There were layers of dust on the windowsills, along with the remains of many insects.

Lisa climbed off the wall and turned around. She looked at the house. Peter copied her; however, he was wondering what his mother had found to look at that was so interesting.

A small front garden, which was once lovingly tended and filled with colour, had turned into neglected wasteland. The weeds had marked their territory after taking over. They were entangled and it was impossible to see where one weed started and another finished as they grew over countless pieces of litter.

Peter looked up at the chimney. He watched as a nesting pigeon was kept busy feeding her noisy family.

"Come on, Peter, it doesn't look like anybody lives here any longer. Let's leave the birds in peace." Lisa wrapped her hand around his and they continued their walk.

They appeared not to have noticed Vicky's mother, Melanie Willis, as she peeked at them from her bedroom window through a gap in the curtains.

Mel had found her existence to be pointless since that fateful day. The day that her daughter was taken away from her and murdered in cold blood. The assailant was never found. Since then, she had become a recluse. She was despondent and hid herself away following the tragedy, where days turned into weeks, which transformed into months and finally into years of solitude.

Despite her being a qualified hairdresser, Mel's hair was a mess. The peroxide had grown out and left a headful of split ends. Her long dark roots exposed greying hairs that were in need of a deep conditioner. Bitten fingernails displayed open sores to each side, where once pristine nails were professionally manicured every month. With no waxing, shaving or pampering of any description she was looking very much worse for wear.

Essential groceries were delivered to Mel's door, maybe once and sometimes twice a month. They always came from the same supermarket, but it was not always the same driver; however, she would always be greeted with the same pitiful expression and on each occasion, she would open the front door just wide enough so that the shopping bags could be placed inside. She would thank them, before closing the door.

Mel was grateful for online shopping. It was her lifeline and a way of communicating with the outside world without having to converse with another living soul, face to face. She would only venture outside when it was essential and during the hours of darkness.

The nearest post box was at the top of her road, which was a short walking distance. In fact, it took Mel longer to put on a pair of shoes than it did to walk to it. She would always allow her mail to mount up before endeavouring to go out as she was afraid that she might bump into someone that she knew.

Junk mail and leaflets created an untidy heap behind Mel's front door and there was more of it scattered along the hall floor. A couple had been posted that morning while the rest was left untouched for what seemed like an age. She would pick up what looked important and then leave it unopened, placing it on an ever-growing pile on the coffee table in the living room.

Vicky had been an only child, Mel's best friend and her whole world. It was obvious that her death had taken it out of her. For years after her late husband, George's, apparent suicide, Mel had taken on the role of both mother and father.

Mel had found Vicky's funeral difficult. It was the last time that she had bothered to make any sort of an effort with her appearance. She'd worn a knee-length black dress, a pair of flat shoes and a blazer style jacket. Her hair was brushed back and tied up. She had moisturised but did not bother to put on any make-up. She had wanted to look her best for her daughter's farewell, but without going over the top and looking like she was on a night out.

Putting the reality of everything that was going on to the back of her mind, Mel had appeared unaware of what was really going on. She had convinced herself that it had all been a mistake and that it was not Vicky's body that had been found at the bottom of the waterfall;

however, despite her denials, reality dawned on her as time went by.

At the funeral, Mel kept turning around to check on the wooden double doors at the back of the church. She had been willing them to open and had wanted Vicky to make one of her grand entrances and say something like, "Mum, there you are. I'm starving. What are you making for our tea, tonight?" or, "Mum, I've been looking everywhere for you. I just wanted to let you know that I'm staying at a friend's house for the night."

Guests were a mixture of bona fide people who knew Vicky, and cared, and wanted to pay their respects, nosey folk who had nothing better to do with their time and were looking for something to gossip about and then there were those who attended so that they could say that they were part of it.

Following the service, Vicky's coffin was lowered into the ground and genuine well-wishers left after they had paid their respects. Mel had ignored the reporters, photographers and camera crew that had lined up to the other side of the road, across from the church. She had stepped out from the grounds of the graveyard and was blinded by the flashes from their cameras. She had looked across at them with a blank expression. Their bombardment of questions had made her head spin. She was not even able to get angry with them for their lack of empathy and had no words to give them that would express how helpless and alone she felt. The overwhelming need she felt to weep would wait until she was back home and away from prying eyes.

Mel watched as Lisa and Peter walked away. *Do I know them?* She shook her head. *No… I don't think I recognise their faces.* She closed the curtain, with care, as she did not want to be noticed.

Turning around, Mel's eyes were drawn to the cover that was draped over the full-length mirror in the corner of her bedroom. *Dare I take a peep at myself?* She took a deep breath, flicked on the light switch and, with trepidation, pulled the cover from off the mirror. She was alarmed by her reflection and it took her only that moment to realise that drastic action needed to be taken. As she ran her fingers through her hair, they were met with numerous tangles. She moved closer to the mirror and said, "Look at yourself, Mel. You look a right bloody mess." Her voice sounded croaky, but it would, as she had not spoken to anyone in a long while. She surveyed her face, turning it from one side to the other. Shaking her head, the shame was evident. "You really have let yourself go, old girl." She became aware of an unpleasant odour. Holding up her left arm, she sniffed at her armpit. She was greeted by a mass of hair and the smell of stale sweat. Pulling her head away, she had a sniff at her other armpit. *Why I thought that one would smell any different is anybody's guess and why the hell didn't I notice before?* She looked at her reflection. "What would George have said to you, Mel? And even more so, *Vicky* for that matter."

Making her way to the bathroom, Mel put the plug into the bath and turned the hot and cold water taps on at the same time. The steam rose and began to fill the room. She undressed and sat on the edge of the bath and looked at her feet. Her toe nails were long and discoloured and the thickened skin on her heels was dry and cracked.

Mel rummaged through the bathroom cabinet and managed to find a disposable razor with minimal traces of rust along the blade. She decided that it would have to do as it looked like it might be up to the job and it was probable that it was the only one that she had.

Turning off the taps, Mel dipped her toes into the water to test its temperature. The warm water was inviting. Not wanting to create a tidal wave, she climbed in with care and lowered herself into the water. As she lay there, allowing herself to soak, her knees protruded. She sat up and reached for the soap that had a number of pubic hairs attached to it. It felt hard, like a rock, and was stuck to the bath top, against the cold-water tap. Scooping some of the warm water into her palms, she poured it over the soap until she managed to loosen it. She laid down and lifted her left leg out of the water and rubbed it over with the soap. The bar of soap softened and began to lather. Her leg hairs sprang through the bubbles. Lowering her leg, she did the same with her right leg. She felt relaxed and started to feel drowsy.

Mel could not be sure if she had drifted off to sleep, but the bath water did feel cooler. She lathered one of her armpits and began to shave, with caution, but the blade clogged and tugged on several of the remaining hairs. She counted to three, held her breath and yanked at the razor. It came free and plucked out some of the attached hairs. She swirled the blade around in the bath water and reached for a pair of scissors. After trimming the hairs on her other armpit, she continued to shave. Where her hair had been, she was left with an angry looking rash. *I think I might need to go and see the nurse to get a tetanus booster for that.*

Unsure if the razor blade would hold out any longer, Mel elevated her left leg and looked at it, with hope. She lathered her shin, shook the razor beneath the water to unclog it and began shaving, but the blade was blunt. It had had enough and made it known when it performed an emergency stop on her shin and took out a lengthy gouge of flesh in the process. Lowering her leg into the bath, the soapy water emphasised her pain. Her eyes watered and she peed a little. She jumped up, shook her leg and shouted, "Bloody hell!" Some of the bathwater flowed over the side. She perched on the edge of the bath, rested the foot of the injured leg to the other side and examined the damage.

Blood trickled down from the open laceration and began reddening the water. With care, Mel attempted to insert the skin, which was still attached at one end, back into the gouge. It was proving to be difficult as it was bloody and not a perfect fit any more.

Reaching over to the side of her, Mel pulled a hand towel from the rail. She pressed it against her wound in an attempt to stem the flow. Wrapping the towel around her leg, she tied it behind her calf. The blood soaked through.

Swivelling her legs, Mel stood up. The soapy water and blood dribbled onto the saturated bathmat. Making her way across the landing, she grabbed her bathrobe from the back of her bedroom door and hobbled down the stairs. She left a bloody trail as she made her way to the first aid box.

Mel sat on the kitchen floor, pulled the lid from the box and rummaged inside for the necessary lint, plasters and bandages. She loosened the towel from around her leg and peeked underneath at the damage. The flow of blood had slowed. Removing the towel, she threw it to one side and inspected her wound. A couple of curly hairs had found their way to the edge of the sore. She attempted to nudge them to one side with the tip of her little finger. One of them moved with ease and she wiped it onto the towel; however, the other needed further persuasion. Delving into the box, she pulled out a pair of tweezers and began picking at the remaining hair. By accident, she pushed it into the inflamed tissue and almost wet herself, but she was determined and pushed the tweezers further into the wound, enduring the severe discomfort until she succeeded in plucking out the hair. Reaching for the towel, she pressed it against the wound until the bleeding had eased. When she had applied the lint and bandage the pain subsided a little.

Throwing the ruined towel to the side of the kitchen bin, Mel made her way up the stairs to the bathroom. She dropped her bathrobe onto the floor, reached into the bathtub, putting her arm through the layer of bloody scum that was on the water's surface and pulled out the plug. Sitting on the side of the bath, she watched and listened as the gurgling water drained away. She pulled along the shower curtain, turned on the shower, put her hand beneath its spray and waited for several seconds until it was warm enough to stand beneath.

The water ran through Mel's matted hair and flowed over her face and body. With her eyes closed, she reached and fumbled until she found the shampoo bottle. She felt for the lid, flicked it open and squeezed a small amount onto the palm of her hand before she massaged it into her hair and scalp.

The bathroom extraction fan was broken, and the room had filled with steam. Mel rinsed away the shampoo and stood for a moment longer as she enjoyed the sensation of the warm water flowing over her skin. For the first time in years, she felt cleansed and more human. Turning off the shower, she pulled the curtain along and climbed out. Picking up her bathrobe from the floor, she put it on. It was two sizes too big as it hung around her. As she made her way to the airing cupboard on the landing, the steam followed as it escaped through the opened door. She reached into the cupboard, grabbed another towel, wrapped it around her hair and went back into the bathroom. The handle on the window was dripping with condensation as she reached to open it.

As Mel turned her head, her attention was drawn to a bright orb that had drifted across the room. It remained still next to the door, as though waiting. Its radiance was stifled by the clearing steam.

Pulling her bathrobe tighter, Mel fastened its sash into a bow. Her heart began to beat faster as she wondered what it was that was in the room with her. She noticed that the bathroom door had been closed. She began to move away. There was no means of escape as the window opener was too small to climb out of, but, for a moment, she still considered it. She sat on the side of the bath.

The orb brightened before it started to change shape and it extended in length quicker than it widened. Its shine began to fade until it was transformed into a human shape. A silhouette moved towards Mel. Be it an illusion or not, she did not care because there in front of her was her daughter, Vicky.

The foul stench of stagnant river water drifted through the air and replaced the gentle soapy aroma. Vicky's colourless complexion and drawn features emphasised the torture she had endured in those last few moments before her death. Her hair was longer and wild with debris collected from the river bed. With her shoulders slumped, she appeared to be struggling to stand as she swayed from side to side. Her tattered dress dripped and created a puddle of red beneath.

Mel was looking at a different Vicky, however. She saw her daughter as she remembered her on that fateful day before she went out with her friends on a picnic. She wiped away her tears with the backs of her fingers and jumped up. "Victoria... my darling," she said as she held out her arms. She wanted to hold her. "Oh, my goodness, sweetheart. I have missed you so much." As she walked towards Vicky, Mel's eyes filled with tears of joy. "Look at you. You look so well."

Vicky remained still. She looked at Mel with a smile that would melt the hardest of souls. "Please help," she mimed before fading.

Rushing towards the door, Mel made a grab for the handle, but her hand slipped away. She tried again and managed to open it. Looking into the landing, she cried out, "Vicky, where are you? I didn't catch what you said. Please come back to me."

The door to Vicky's bedroom was ajar. It was always kept closed. Mel walked towards the room and pushed the door. The room was empty of life, but she had a feeling that it would be. In fact, the whole house felt deserted and lifeless. She had not noticed before.

Mel stepped inside Vicky's bedroom and sat on the dressing table stool. She looked around the room. It was the same as when Vicky had last slept there. Items of clothing lay where they had been thrown or dropped. The bed looked untidy with the duvet bunched up in the middle and the pillow was squashed where she had laid her head. Layers of dust covered opened bottles of perfumes, cans of deodorant and hairspray aerosols. Most were missing lids, and some lay on their sides, along with dried up face creams and an assortment of nail varnishes, and with make-up left scattered on her dressing table it looked every inch a typical young lady's bedroom. Mel picked up a hairbrush and noticed Vicky's blonde hairs attached. There was a dust free patch on the dressing table where the brush had been. She began brushing her wet hair and tugged through the lugs. Gathering a clump of hair between her thumb and index finger, she pulled it forward to look at it. There were many split ends.

Mel woke early the next morning. It was dark outside. She was lying on the duvet of Vicky's bed. She had only meant to rest her eyes for a few minutes and had somehow managed to sleep right through the night. *I might as well go and make myself an early breakfast.*

Mel sat at the kitchen table with a cup of black coffee and a slice of dry toast. *Vicky came to visit me yesterday to assure me that everything's going to be all right.* She nodded and smiled to herself. *My daughter's watching over me. I think she wants me to move on with my life.*

Mel looked at the overflowing sink. *Time to make a start on the cleaning.* All the crockery, cutlery and pans that she owned were stacked on the drainer. She emptied the sink and washed and dried every item before she made her way to the bathroom to freshen up.

A cool breeze caught Mel by surprise as it blew over her face. She noticed that the bathroom window was open from the day before. With her toothbrush gripped between her teeth, she reached and closed it. Gargling the last of the mouthwash, she spat it into the washbasin.

A pink scrunchie, which was lying on the floor, caught Mel's attention. She picked it up. As her fingertips touched it, a distant memory came flooding back. Squeezing it, she remembered the day that she had bought a similar one for Vicky, who had been a little girl at the time.

While out shopping, Mel and Vicky had called into the local pharmacy in Beechwood to pick up a prescription for George. Vicky had seen an assortment of coloured scrunchies on the counter inside a transparent tub and wanted one. Pink was her favourite colour. She began pleading with Mel and it did not take much time before she had managed to persuade her to buy her one. Vicky had held her hand out and looked up with an angelic expression. Mel pulled her purse out of her pocket, looked through it and picked out the right amount of change before placing it, one coin at a time, into Vicky's palm. Vicky was not able to contain her excitement as she jumped up and down and nearly dropped the money. She got herself under control, remained still and kept hold of every coin by making a fist around them.

Vicky began pleading with Mel before they had managed to get out of the pharmacy. She made it seem like it was essential that she wore the scrunchie without delay, as if the whole existence of the universe depended on it. As they got outside, it began to rain and the drops bounced off every surface they came into contact with.

With her shopping bags in one hand, Mel grabbed Vicky with the other and bundled her under her arm. The two of them had to make a run for it. She could not see where she was going as the rain hit her in the face. Vicky, who was looking towards the ground, was unaware of Mel's struggle and giggled as she bounced up and down. They managed to find shelter inside an old wooden bus stop. The roof leaked and the window was smashed, but they were out of the rain. Mel put her shopping onto the seat before she put a wriggling Vicky down.

Drenched, Mel panted for breath, while Vicky continued to smile, even though she was shivering. Reaching into the bottom of her cluttered handbag, Mel retrieved a hairbrush and with the scrunchie gripped between her lips, she began to put the brush through Vicky's hair and gathered it into a ponytail. Vicky squealed with delight and hugged Mel. The two of them waited until the rain had stopped before they made their way home.

Opening her hand, Mel looked at the scrunchie. *This is brand new. It can't be the same one that Vicky had. Hers was filthy and it'd lost its elasticity. I can remember her wearing it every single day for months and then she got cross with me when I told her that I'd thrown it in the bin.* Mel put the scrunchie on the washbasin and made her way to her bedroom.

Mel was going to have a long overdue pampering day but would need to go into the local town because the village did not have any such amenities. She put on a clean pair of jeans as she needed to cover up her half shaven legs and fresh wound. After spraying a quick squirt of deodorant onto each armpit, which stung, she grabbed a tee shirt and pulled it over her head.

Rummaging through her cosmetics bag, Mel found a bottle of mascara that she had not opened. Most of the other make-up was unusable. She removed the mascara's plastic packaging, unscrewed the lid, looked into a compact mirror and started to apply the mascara to her lashes.

Mel put on a pair of trainers and grabbed a jacket from the hall. Opening the front door, she stepped outside into the daylight. The sunlight dazzled her. She turned and went back indoors. The brightness continued to shine through into the hall and emphasised the dust particles that were hovering in the air. While reflecting back to Vicky's visit the previous day, Mel found her sunglasses in a top drawer of the cabinet. She put them on and felt ready to take on the world.

Striding through the village, Mel noticed that things had not changed since she had last ventured out beyond the realms of her road. Village life had managed to continue without her. Unfamiliar faces popped up, in amongst the recognisable ones. Some smiled while others looked through her. Nevertheless, she was grateful that nobody appeared to be pointing or whispering about her any more. *Thank God that people have got short memories and that I'm yesterday's news.*

Beechwood train station was deserted when Mel arrived. Rush hour commuters had long since left and would be sitting at their desks staring at their computer monitors, like programmed robots, for the remainder of the working day. The sound of traffic from the main road could be heard in the distance. Surrounding trees rustled in the breeze as they tilted together in the same direction and swayed as though showing off their natural splendour. Walking into the shelter, she looked around for a timetable. The shelter looked like it had been painted and was, for the time being, graffiti free. There wasn't a noticeboard and if it weren't for the shelter being there, there were no other clues to suggest that a train ever stopped at the station.

Mel strolled outside onto the platform and crossed over the yellow line marker. Standing next to the platform edge, she looked at the railway line. Clumps of dried toilet paper were stuck, at random, to the track with glass and plastic bottles scattered alongside. There was no sign of an approaching train in the distance.

Mel walked into the shelter. It smelt of fresh paint, but there weren't any 'wet paint' signs. She checked anyway and poked her index finger against the metal seat. It felt dry. She sat and began to wait for the next train to arrive.

Catching sight of her own reflection in the window, Mel could not help but stare. She did not recognise the older and thinner person that looked back at her. She had lost a lot of weight and although she looked frail, she did not feel unwell.

"Good morning," said the priest. He was an elderly gentleman who was light on his feet. He had joined Mel in the shelter and was standing next to her. He was a distinguished looking chap who for some unexplainable reason appeared to look out of place. His whole demeanour gave the impression that he had somehow slipped into and got lost in the wrong era.

Mel was no longer in a daze as she jumped to her feet. "Good morning," she said before sitting again, as though a length of her knickers' elastic had got stuck on the bench.

"Apologies for alarming you. That most certainly was not my intention." The priest appeared to bow. He revealed a centre parting in a full head of white hair. Introducing himself, he held out an aged hand. "Damian Ponder," he said with an air of confidence.

Taking his hand, Mel noted that Damian had a gentle handshake. "That's okay. I was in a world of my own. I never even heard you coming." She remembered that she had not made it known what her name was, so she continued, "I'm Melanie Willis."

"May I sit down next to you, Melanie?" Damian's natural old-fashioned charm and manners were exemplary. He did not want to make any assumptions and so he stood next to her, smiled and waited for her to respond.

Mel slid along the bench and said, "Oh yes... of course, please do." She gestured for Damian to sit next to her.

During the silence that followed, she thought about why she had needed to make room for him, as they were, after all, the only two people in the whole of the station and the bench ran the entire length of the shelter.

Damian looked up at the sky. He began to examine each wispy cloud. "It looks like it's going to be a pleasant day."

Feeling relaxed in Damian's company, Mel was satisfied that he did not seem bothered by her unkempt appearance.

"Are you new to the area, Damian?" She tried to speak with a posher accent. "It's just that I don't think I've seen you about before. I'm sure I would have remembered if I had."

Damian turned to look at Mel and said, "I'm just passing through. You sure live in a beautiful part of the world."

The platform's wooden planks vibrated beneath as a train passed them on the furthest track. Both of them watched until it was no longer in view. Peace resumed. "Are you going anywhere nice today?"

"Just into town. I'm not going anywhere special." Mel pointed at her hair and emphasised the condition of it by giving a disapproving look. "I think a trip to the hairdressers is well overdue. As you've probably already guessed, it's been a while since I had my hair done."

Without warning, another train sped past. This time, though, it was on the nearest track, but it was going in the opposite direction. Mel and Damian watched it until it was out of view. "If you don't mind me asking, what is it that you do for a living, Mel?"

"No, I don't mind." Mel smiled. *How lovely the world would be if there were more people like Damian in it.* "I don't do anything... well, not at the moment. Although, I'm a qualified hairdresser with many years of experience. More than I'd care to remember." Mel chuckled. *I haven't really given it much thought lately, but I think that I've missed hairdressing.* "I left my job several weeks after my daughter passed away. I was having way too much time off work. I was depressed. I'd worked at a salon in town for years, but it was only going to be a matter of time before they gave me the push." She felt an overpowering urge to pour her heart out to this man that she had never seen before.

"I'm sorry to hear about all the sadness that you have had to suffer." Damian hesitated before he continued. He was thinking about what he was going to

146

say next, as he did not want to put her through any more upset. "I can only imagine the pain you have had to endure, and by yourself too. Have you learnt to live with your grief and are you ready to do battle with the world once again?"

Mel shrugged. "I think so, but I'm not entirely sure. I suppose that if I don't do it now, then I'm never going to do it, am I?"

"I never had any children of my own, but I have experienced loss, a great many times. You never truly get over it. You just learn to live with it and try to get on with your life, the best that you can." Damian glanced up at the sky before he looked at Mel. "Do you think that you will go back into hairdressing? It might help you to be around other people."

Mel also looked up at the sky and considered how each passing moment was a changing picture and that no two views were ever the same. She looked at Damian and smiled. *It was destiny that made our paths cross today.* "If I'm being honest, I just don't know. I think I'm going to take each day as it comes, starting from today."

"Have you ever thought of working for yourself?"

Mel did not respond.

"I'm only bringing up the subject because I noticed that there's a premises in your village that looks like it might be available. They were clearing it out when I went by. It looks like it might have been some kind of junk shop. It would make an ideal salon for you, being so close to home and I could picture you running it."

Mel shrugged. Her mind and heart were confused. "Oh, I don't know," she sighed. "It would be so much hard work."

"Yes, it would, but don't you think that it would be worth it? Just think how proud George and Vicky would be." Damian wanted to give Mel some time to absorb the idea. "Oh well, it was just an idea and something for you to think about." He got to his feet and looked around. "It most definitely is a beautiful day."

Mel could see a train heading towards them. It began to slow down and its brakes screeched along the track. "I think this is our train," she said. "Thank you, Damian. It was so lovely to meet you. I do hope that we bump into each other again, and soon."

"You are more than welcome. The pleasure was all mine." Damian winked before he continued, "Always remember that there are some good souls out there that will be only too happy to help you."

Mel walked towards the platform edge. *Hang on a minute! How did Damian know that I was alone when my daughter died? And how did he know what Vicky and George's names were? I didn't mention any of that to him in our conversation.* She turned to ask him. The sound of a pre-recorded message bellowed out of the speaker above her. It was announcing the train's imminent arrival. Several other passengers were standing close behind her. There were working mothers

148

who had dropped their children off at school and stay-at-home mothers with pushchairs. *Where did all these people come from? Have they just arrived, or have they been here all the time?* She examined each face, but to no avail. Damian was not on the platform or in the shelter. *Where did he go?*

The train stopped and fear rushed through Mel. *Oh shit! Do I get on this train or do I go home and hide myself away, just for a little while longer? I can always try again another day.*

One of the carriage doors opened right in front of Mel. She moved sideways to allow an elderly lady to alight. The lady was frail on her feet as she gripped the handrail. She lowered her rickety legs onto the platform. Mel watched her, as she was mindful that the gap between the train and the platform was large enough for the lady to fall into, but she made it without injury and stood on the platform, clear of the train doors and gap.

The passengers behind Mel began shoving her. They were unaware of her dilemma, but they had made the decision for her as they pushed her aboard the train. *I'll look silly if I get off now.*

Mel sat in the hairdresser's chair and watched the chaos going on behind her, through the reflection in the mirror. Her hairdresser's name was Sally. She looked fresh out of college. She advised Mel to have a 'bob' style and Mel agreed with her suggestion. During the silent pauses in conversation, she watched as Sally snipped away at her hair. *Would I be able to run a salon of my own?* That chat she'd had with Damian earlier had given her plenty to think about.

It was some hours later when Mel made the return train journey home, but not before she had managed to fit in a visit to a beauty salon and a nail bar. She even found the time to purchase some razors. The train was quiet as it was not quite the evening rush hour. Most of the regular commuters would still be toiling at their places of work. She sat by a window that faced forward. The conductor appeared at her side and checked that her travel ticket was valid. The train set off.

Mel watched pheasants and rabbits as they ran about on the rolling hills. As the train approached Beechwood Station, a fox that was near to the train track changed direction and made its way stealthily through the trees.

While strolling home through the village, Mel felt something digging into her heel. She placed her bag onto the ground and propped her foot onto a windowsill ledge, unfastened the lace and pulled off her trainer. Balancing on her other foot, she shook the trainer and watched as a small stone flew out. She put the trainer back on and fastened the lace into a bow.

Mel looked up at the signage on the shop that she was standing outside of. *What are the chances?* It was the empty junk shop that Damian had mentioned earlier! *Is it fate or coincidence that I just happen to stop right outside?*

Pressing her nose against the window, Mel could visualise what it could look like. She felt a twinge of excitement. All the furnishings would be of shabby chic design and of the finest quality. Customers would be greeted by a warm and welcoming face which would look up at them, from behind a curved reception desk, as they entered. Backwash units would be to the rear of the salon while the styling units and chairs would be to both sides with a couple in the middle of the room. Waiting customers would sit with their backs to the window and read the latest copies of the trendiest magazines. It would be busy with the finest stylists who would always be helpful. *It's definitely going to need a lot of work doing to it before it looks anything like I imagine, but I'm ready for something to fill my time and I feel ready for the challenge.*

The self-imposed confinement in her house had played a part in making Mel feel like a prisoner, but now she was liberated. The house was too big for one person alone to be living and pottering around in. She had come to terms with the fact that George and Vicky would never return; however, she believed that they were both watching over her, but it was time for her to move on and allow them both to rest in peace.

Mel reminisced while she took her time sorting through Vicky's bedroom. Anything sentimental – and there was plenty – was placed inside a cardboard box. Everything else was either thrown out or donated to the charity shop.

Beechwood Skip Hire arrived on time and placed a maxi-skip on the road outside Mel's house. Barricade lights hung from traffic cones to each corner of the skip. *That'll get the neighbours' nets twitching and give them something to talk about.* Over the next few days she filled it with rubbish from the house and with the overgrown weeds and litter that were in her garden. She turned a blind eye to items that were thrown in there, during the hours of darkness, by the neighbours without a please or a thank you.

Mel was exhausted after hours of spring cleaning. She felt happy that the house was ready to put onto the market and never gave staying there any longer a second thought.

A couple of viewers had passed over the threshold before the house sold for the full asking price. The estate agent had not even had chance to put up the 'for sale' board. Mel was satisfied that the house was going to be the property of a young couple who were smitten with the place as soon as they walked through the front door.

After a couple of days of haggling with another estate agent, a price was agreed for both the shop and the flat above it. Mel moved into the flat within a couple of months and began spring cleaning what would become her new home. It would need refurbishing, but that would have to wait until a later date as most of her money would need to be put into her new business.

Mel found a local company to do the refurbishment work on her hair salon. Their offices were located beneath the railway viaduct, to the opposite end of the village. Initial meetings took place to discuss the project plans, how the workmen were going to keep disturbances to a minimum and all the other boring health and safety 'mumbo jumbo' that went with it. Local villagers had taken note that something was going on when they saw a works van parked outside. Word soon got out that changes were afoot.

Beechwood Skip Hire placed a skip outside Mel's new premises. A couple of young men began dismantling the shelving inside the shop and storeroom. They placed the longer pieces of wood, upright and around the edges of the skip.

Mel was standing several feet from the shop door. Taking a breather and leaning against the shop window, she was trying not to get under the workmen's feet as they filled the skip.

"Mel?"

That voice sounds familiar. But Mel was not sure if she was ready for all the questions. She looked and smiled through almost gritted teeth. "Linda, how are you?"

Linda gave Mel a brief hug. "Oh, I'm good. You know me. I could grumble, but I doubt anyone would bother to listen." She reached into her jacket pocket and pulled out a squashed cigarette packet while she fumbled in her other pockets for her lighter. She chuckled to herself and rolled her eyes when she managed to find it. "It feels like I haven't seen you in ages." Her facial expression turned to one of sympathy. "How are you feeling?" Her tone sounded patronising.

There's no denying it. I do feel good again. In fact, it's the best that I've felt for quite some time and, what's more, I don't even feel guilty about it. "I think I'm getting there. Thanks for asking. It's nice to know that people still care. I've had a bit of a tough time of it, but I'm sure that everybody is already aware of that." Mel paused for a moment before she continued, "Do you know what though? It's time that I stopped wallowing in self-pity and grabbed life with both hands again. I need to move on and that's exactly what I'm doing. I feel it's the right time for me to be doing something with my life again and it wouldn't hurt if my bank balance got a lift in the long run, too."

Linda was listening to Mel's every word as she put a cigarette to her lips. "I did call round at yours a few times when I was passing, but I didn't want to keep knocking. I just assumed that you didn't answer because you wanted to be left alone." She held the lighter to the cigarette, but it did not ignite. She shook the lighter and after several attempts a weak flame appeared and lit the tip of her cigarette on one side.

Strange, I don't recall anyone bothering to take the time to knock on my door. When I think about it, there wasn't one message left on the answering machine or a missed call on my mobile, either. "Sorry, Linda, I never heard anything. I would have let you in and made you a cuppa if I had."

"Oh, don't worry about it. You might have been taking a call of nature or something and it was a long time ago." Linda could feel the awkwardness of the conversation and changed the subject. "Anyway, I've heard that we're actually going to be getting a hair salon in the village. How exciting for you and for us." She took a drag on her cigarette, inhaled the smoke and continued, "By the way, did you hear about Fred?" Residual smoke escaped from her mouth and nostrils as she spoke.

"Fred?" Mel felt the need to say his name out loud as though it would help her to remember him. She looked at Linda and waited for her to give her further clues, but she did not need any because she only knew the one Fred. "Do you mean the old man that used to own this shop before it became vacant?"

Linda nodded and waited until the two workmen were inside the shop before she continued, "Yes, that's him. The 'junk shop man' as we used to call him." She looked around to check that there was no one else listening.

"No, I've not heard anything. What about him?" *To be honest, I've not even given Fred a second thought.*

Linda inhaled on her cigarette. "Some young men found him in his shop. It's been quite busy in there these last few years because..." She stopped mid-sentence when she remembered who she was talking to and who she was about to start gossiping about. Her voice quietened and her mouth movements became exaggerated as she continued, "Well, anyway, never mind about all that. The young men found him lying in a heap on the floor of the storeroom. He'd passed away."

Mel noticed that Linda's two top middle teeth were stained with nicotine. She could not stop herself from staring at them. *I thought she was going to say that he'd retired to the Algarve or somewhere.* "Oh no, that's just awful and so sad." She felt sorry and tried to imagine what it must have been like for him, dying alone. *That means I'm standing just several feet away from where Fred spent his final moments.* She began to feel uncomfortable about the conversation.

"The young men looked ever such a nice group. I think they were goths. Do you know the ones that I mean? They like to dress all in black and have very pale faces. I watched them as they walked into Fred's shop." Linda took another drag on her cigarette. It was burnt down to the filter. Her facial expression revealed that she had more to tell. "The funny thing is, though, they walked in and it was only a matter of minutes before an ambulance arrived. Of course, I went over to see if I could help with anything, but I couldn't get past the door; however, I did manage to grab one of the paramedics. He explained that whoever it was that had rung must have known him personally because they knew his full name, date of birth and the cause of death."

Mel was distracted by the comings and goings of the two workmen. Both of them were working up a sweat as they continued to fill the skip without taking a break. Her mind wandered momentarily as she estimated how long it would be before it was full.

It was silent. Linda had stopped talking.

Did I miss something? "Sorry, Linda. I'm not following. Why is that a funny thing?"

Linda was oblivious to Mel's lapse of concentration. She was happy that she had someone to tell the story to that had not heard it before. "Because I told the paramedic it must have been one of the young men that had entered the shop."

"And?" Mel was still missing the point.

"Well, I was stood outside the whole time because I was having a fag break. The goth group went in. The ambulance arrived. Two paramedics went in." Linda inhaled on her cigarette. It was burning through the filter and must have tasted awful. "The paramedic told me that when they arrived there was no one in the shop apart from Fred. I know that I saw the young men definitely go in, but they never came out through the shop door. Apparently, they couldn't have got out the back way, either, because it was blocked off by a pile of boxes."

"Oh my God! Who the hell were they?" Mel's mouth was gaping.

Linda had given plenty of thought to who the young men could have been, but always came to the same conclusion. "It just as to be something to do with the paranormal; however, I can't be one hundred percent sure, but what other explanation could there be?"

Mel did not answer. She turned to look through the window and beyond the open storeroom door at the back. She tried to imagine where Fred had died. *Poor soul, but am I now the owner of a haunted building? I wish I'd known before I bought it.*

"Goodness me, look at the time." Linda looked at her wristwatch. She threw her cigarette end onto the ground, stamped her foot down and flattened it. "I'd best get back to the shop. My break was over ten minutes ago." She began to walk away but stopped and turned around with an afterthought. "It was so lovely to see you again and have a bit of a catch up. We must do it again soon." She smiled. "Do you know what makes it really sad though?"

Mel said nothing. *I'm not even going to hazard a guess.* She looked at Linda with a blank expression as she waited for her to continue.

"Fred died on the same day that he was supposed to start his retirement. There was a group of us having a few drinks and nibbles with him, just before he died. He went into the storeroom and locked the door behind him. We all decided to leave because we presumed that he'd had enough and just wanted some peace and quiet. We never thought for one minute that he'd gone in there to die." Linda shrugged. There was a gap in the traffic. She crossed the road and without turning, she waved and hurried back into the charity shop.

Chapter Ten
Limbo

Fred found himself gazing through the window of a shop that looked familiar. It looked like it was in the process of being refurbished into a hair salon. He turned and looked around the village. *All the other shops still look the same. And, when did all that snow go?* He stepped away from the window and looked up at the sign. *What the hell's going on? That's my shop. I knew it was. I must have forgotten to lock the door when I went out for a walk and now squatters have moved in.* He pulled down on the handle and pushed against the door, but it would not budge. *Someone else must have locked it.* He tried his key in the keyhole, but it would not fit. The key was too big for the narrow slot. In fact, not only was the handle different, but so was the door. This did not deter him from trying the key, over and over again, until he admitted defeat.

Pressing his face against the window, Fred could see that there were no longer any of his collectibles inside or any evidence that it had been a junk shop. *What the hell's going on?* He sat on the doorstep and sighed. Resting his elbows on his knees, he propped his chin onto the palms of his hands and stared at the ground.

Why can't I get in? My whole life's in that building. What am I supposed to do now? Should I call the police? And where is everyone? I'll wait here until someone comes and then maybe I can get some answers.

The two elderly ladies walked by. They had not noticed Fred sitting on the doorstep. He had not heard that vehicle braking or seen its headlights, but his attention had been elsewhere. He got to his feet and shouted after them, "Excuse me, ladies. I wonder if you can help me."

Neither of the ladies replied and continued with their conversation, but they appeared oblivious to its repetition.

Fred followed the ladies up the hill but kept his distance from them. He did not want to alarm them if they were to turn around. He looked at the ground when he thought that he had spotted a silver coin, but there wasn't anything there and when he looked up again, he found himself standing outside the door of the hair salon. *It would seem that I'm also on some type of a time loop, but why am I the only one that appears to have noticed what's going on?* He sat and watched as the ladies crossed the road and walked past him, over and over again.

Unexpectedly, the madness stopped, and it was followed by silence. A shaft of white light appeared with a radiance similar to nothing that Fred had witnessed before. It was brilliant, but at the same time not dazzling or blinding. A warmth passed through his body. It felt similar to stepping indoors after being outside in the cold air for a long period. The glow expanded and a distant figure emerged as though it was moving towards him from the end of a tunnel. The silhouette was that of a female shape. She moved nearer until her face became clear. She held out her arms and smiled. He rubbed his eyes and checked. Yes, it was Katherine.

All Fred could do was stare. He was afraid to look away or blink. *Katherine, please don't be a figment of my imagination. Don't vanish.* She looked the same as he remembered. "Katherine, is that really you?"

Katherine put her arms by her sides and tilted her head to one side. "Yes, Fred, it's really me." Her voice was gentle. "You must feel like it was a lifetime ago since we were together." She regarded how old he looked. His hair was thinner and had greyed. Wrinkles cut deep around his eyes, surrounded his mouth and remained on his brow. His time had passed slower than hers. "I'm so sorry that I left you behind to cope with everything by yourself."

"You broke my heart. Not just because you left me behind, but because you never told me how you felt." He considered how young she looked. He turned to look at his reflection in the window, but he could not see himself or Katherine. Where they stood were two orbs of light floating in the air.

"I loved you and Peter." Katherine paused before she continued, "you have to know that, and I still do."

"It was the worst day of my life when I found your body." Fred closed his eyes. He could still visualise Katherine's lifeless body laid on their bed. An empty vodka bottle lay on its side on the bedside table and several empty painkiller blister packs were on the carpet next to the bed. Her body had tried to reject them, but she had choked to death on her vomit.

"I wasn't able to talk about how I felt. I was a failure. I couldn't cope with that life and I didn't want to. I was in a bad place. I know that sounds blasé, but I can't undo what's done." Katherine was aware of Fred's distress, but it was time for them both to move on. "You did a fine job without me, though." She paused and smiled. "Are you ready, Fred?"

Fred held out his hand. "I've been ready since the day you died."

Katherine and Fred sat in silence in Beechwood Park. Shafts of the deepest blue light beamed down onto the wild flowers and shrubbery that blanketed the ground. Clouds of the purest white drifted across the sky.

The sounds of a creaking swing and excited children playing could be heard several feet away, but Katherine and Fred were not able to see them. An apparent downpour caught the children by surprise and caused their shocked screams to fill the air, but Katherine and Fred could not see or feel the rain.

Katherine looked at Fred and noted his expression of awe. "Do you know where you are?"

Fred did not answer, but he did nod his head. *This must be heaven.* He got to his feet, looked behind him and noticed the sycamore tree. While all trees looked the same to most people, he was familiar with that particular one. He placed his hands onto the tree and tried to feel around for the carved pentangle, but rather than being greeted by its rough bark, his hands disappeared inside its trunk.

Katherine had joined Fred and was standing by his side. "I watched over you and waited until we could be together again."

Fred did not answer.

I know that Fred isn't listening to me. It's probably all just a little bit too overwhelming for him. He just needs more time to come to terms with everything that's happening.

Fred pulled his hands from the trunk and examined them. Both were intact, but he double-checked to be sure. *This is all because of that photograph I found earlier of Katherine and Peter. It's triggered some memories and is causing me to have this dream. Of course, I want to be with my family again, but what are the chances?* He closed his eyes, focused on his big comfortable bed at home and tried to wake himself from his dream.

A noise came from inside the tree. It sounded similar to someone walking through a pile of dried leaves. Fred opened his eyes, took several steps back and watched as the figure of a man appeared from the trunk. He recognised him. It was their son, Peter; however, unlike Katherine, he did not look the same as the last time he had seen him. He looked ill with a colourless complexion and had the eyes of someone who had not slept for months; they were bloodshot within their darkened sockets.

Peter did not seem to be surprised to see Fred standing in front of him. "Dad, it's so good to have you here. It's been way too long, hasn't it?"

"Am I dreaming? Please tell me that I'm not going to wake up." Fred looked Peter up and down. He noted that he was wearing the same suit that was on the missing person's poster.

Katherine remembered asking herself that same question when she first arrived, but there had been no one waiting for her. She smiled and said, "No, you're not dreaming."

"So, that must mean that I'm dead." Fred inspected himself. *I can still see myself though. I thought I'd be a ball of light or see through, but why would I be? Katherine and Peter aren't.* "I don't feel any of my usual aches and pains. They all appear to have gone and this place sure feels like it could be heaven."

Katherine paused before she answered. She liked that despite all the heartache that Fred had gone through, he had not changed over the years. "Well, it is, and it isn't. Nobody really dies, you see. You just leave your old shell behind, but your energy moves on."

Fred turned to look at Peter. "Are you going to be staying with us too, Son?"

"Not yet. I just wanted to come and say hello to both of you." Peter reached to touch Fred, but his hand passed through his arm.

"Jesus, Peter, you're a flaming ghost." Fred looked at Katherine. "Does that mean that you're a ghost too? Oh, Lord... that must mean that I am! Am I a ghost?" *Come on... calm yourself down.*

Katherine's voice remained calm, "Yes, if you like."

Fred turned to Peter. "Anyway, what do you mean 'not yet'?"

"I've got some unfinished business that I need to take care of. I want to make sure that my family are going to be okay before I can join you on, shall we say, a more permanent basis," Peter said in his usual confident manner.

"Now, Peter, there comes a time in your life when you have to let them go. Allow them to make their own mistakes, no matter how bad it may seem," Fred said. *This all feels a little too surreal. I haven't given my son any advice in a very long time.*

Peter chuckled. "In your life?" *That's funny, Dad.* He shook his head. "You never let me go or gave up on me. Well, I won't give up on mine either."

He's absolutely right. Fred paused for a moment before asking, "But what I don't understand is, how can you help them when you're not even physically there?"

165

"Oh, you'd be surprised what I'm capable of doing." Peter laughed, turned and disappeared into the tree.

Fred tried to follow him but found himself walking through the tree and back out to the opposite side. He peeked around the tree trunk.

Katherine was shaking her head. "What are you trying to do?" She failed to hide her amusement.

Fred's facial expression changed to mirror Katherine's. He did not answer, but started to ask questions of his own, "Why did that just happen? And where did Peter go?"

Katherine sat and patted the grass to the side of her. "Come and sit next to me, Fred. There is so much that I need to tell you." She did not need to ask him twice. "That is where our son died. He was brutally murdered against that very tree." She pointed at the sycamore.

"Murdered! By whom?" Fred shouted. "There wasn't a single day went by when I didn't think about our Peter. Where he was. What he was doing or if something had happened to him."

"I know." Katherine knew that Fred was angry, but she felt that it was necessary for him to hear the truth. "I listened as that George Willis and John Parkins butchered our son and there was absolutely *nothing* I could do to stop them. I was powerless to help. I tried to get to him, but I couldn't. Something held me back."

"George and John! The murdering bastards. They were meant to be friends. Why did they kill him?" Fred lowered his head. "Oh, Katherine, I don't blame you for anything that's happened. I just cherished the time that I got to spend with Peter of an evening. Did they kill him because he got involved with Elizabeth? She was already courting John, you see. I said nothing and didn't interfere. She went on to have a little girl, Lisa, our granddaughter… I did report Peter as missing, but part of me hoped that he'd just moved away to avoid any trouble. I just assumed that one day he'd get in touch when it had all calmed down. Now I know why he didn't. It was because he couldn't."

"I know that the two of you were very close. I just wish I'd found the strength to carry on, so that I could have been with you both and then none of this would have happened."

"I know." Fred could see the regret in Elizabeth's eyes. *I just wish I'd known what George and John had done to our son. I'd have killed the bastards with my bare hands.*

"Your portal to go back is wherever you die. It doesn't matter if your death is from natural causes, suicide or murder. Most souls choose to move on, but for others, like me, it wasn't quite that easy. The moment I swallowed those pills I realised that I'd made a mistake and I had to be sure that you were okay. Our son is just doing the same with Lisa and Peter, our great-grandson. He does come and go a lot to see me, but what he doesn't know is that I know what attaches itself to him each time he goes back. I know that there is always

167

a black shadow waiting in the tree for him." Katherine paused before she began to talk about the cult's actions. "Each night when you did that devil worshipping thing, that black shadow watched over you all. It was like it was waiting for something to happen. It took a particular interest in Peter because of his zest for life more than likely. It was elated when he was the one that was murdered, and it instantly attached itself to him."

"I had no idea that we were devil worshipping. George told us that it was a way of communicating with spirits in the afterlife. All I ever wanted to do was to talk to you. He told us all that he had a special gift, a psychic power if you like, and through him we could talk to anyone that had passed over to the other side. Eventually, he'd hoped that he could make a career out of it and make some easy cash for himself and his family. Maybe he could even get himself onto the telly." Fred looked at Katherine. *I wonder if she believes what I'm telling her.* "What exactly is this black shadow that attaches itself to Peter? Have you any idea?"

Katherine moved away from the tree. Fred followed and walked by her side. Afraid that the black shadow might overhear her, she moved her mouth closer to his ear as she spoke, "I don't know exactly, but whatever it is, I know for certain that it's hostile. The plants surrounding the sycamore always wither when it's near. Didn't you notice?"

Fred shook his head. "George was found dead. Rumour had it that he'd committed suicide. He was found hanging from one of the trees in this park. I always found it hard to believe that he would have taken his own life. He always appeared to have everything in his life so under control." He turned to look at the sycamore and its surrounding plants. They weren't wilted any more. "John died from a massive heart attack. Do you know, I was so upset when I heard about the two of them dying? Now, I'm hoping that each of them had a slow painful death. Hang on... do you think that there's some kind of connection between our son's murder and them two dying?" He did not give Katherine time to answer. "Have you seen either of them since?"

Katherine's facial expression had changed to one of concern. "Please don't be angry. I know it's difficult, but you need to leave all the animosity behind."

"I just need a little more time to process everything that's happened." Fred did not look calm. "Do you think that Peter knows about that black shadow that attaches itself to him?"

"I assume that he does, but I don't really know. Peter never goes into detail about what he does when he goes back through. I did ask him once, but he told me that he's just looking out for his family and he will do absolutely anything necessary to protect them. He won't allow anyone to hurt them." Katherine's smile returned as she began to explain how grateful she felt. "Even though I was never there for him while he grew into such a fine young man, he came to me as soon as he died. He knew exactly who I was. He's never once pointed the finger of blame or questioned why I left him behind."

Fred took a moment to reflect. "Peter did us proud, didn't he?" He remembered the incident that took place in his storeroom. "I had the most frightening experience in my shop with some sort of entity. I'd forgotten all about it until you mentioned that black shadow. God knows how. It was trying to fly away with me until Peter ordered it to stop. I didn't see him, but it was definitely his voice that I heard. Do you know anything about it?"

"It could have been one of many. Each world is full of evil spirits and some aren't always in demon form." Katherine changed the subject. "I used to come and watch you."

"Did you? I wish I'd known that you were there. I wouldn't have felt so lonely."

"When you were sleeping, I'd lay by your side. You were always such a restless sleeper and don't get me started on your snoring and fidgeting," Katherine laughed. "I'd come and watch you working in your shop. You'd always chat away to your regulars, make endless cups of teas and eat the same food for your lunch every day. I know you enjoyed your little empire, but when you were alone, I did realise how lonely you were because you would stare out of the window with such a glum expression."

That's why I sometimes caught the smell of her perfume. It wasn't my imagination. "My world seemed to stand still without you."

"I can't put into words just how sorry I am, Fred, but you don't need to be lonely any more because we're together again. Time seems to go much quicker here, but you'll soon discover that for yourself. Are you ready? I've got so much to show you."

Chapter Eleven
Mr & Mrs Mole

Lisa had looked around various houses over the months that followed, but not one of them felt right. They were either too small, in the wrong location or needed too much work doing to them. She was starting to get concerned that she was never going to find the right house and she needed to find a job because living in a hotel was beginning to put a strain on her bank balance.

After breakfast, Lisa and Peter went out for one of their walks. This routine was getting to be a bit tedious for both of them. They found themselves heading towards her old family home, but this time, they decided to go via a different route.

Everything appears smaller than what I remember and why has so much been left to deteriorate? I wonder why I've never noticed before. There was a subsiding garage with its door unable to close and it was being suffocated by rampant ivy. Lisa and Peter passed an old rusty car. It was hard to tell if it had been parked in the bush or if the bush had grown around it. Its windows were smashed, tyres deflated, upholstery ripped up and it was covered in a generous coating of bird shit. It appeared that the local council had forgotten about some of the village's roads. There were dirt drifts against the kerbs with splinters of wood, nails and squashed plastic bottles. Garden gates were hanging off their hinges and there were countless neglected gardens and curtains closed during daylight hours.

"Turn your head," Lisa said to Peter, as they walked past a fresh piece of road kill. A ginger cat lay lifeless to the side of the road with its mouth open. Its tongue was sticking out and was fixed in place by its teeth. Both of its eyeballs had popped out of their sockets, but there was only a small amount of blood.

Peter ignored his mother's request and bent over to get a better look. He reached to poke it with his finger, but Lisa grabbed his arm and pulled him away. "Yuck... come on, Peter. Don't touch it. That thing will be riddled with germs." They walked a little further before she stopped and pointed to the other side of the road through the trees. She could see someone through the window, pottering about in the front room. "That's where I grew up, Peter."

"I know." Peter looked across the road before he glanced behind him. He found the remains of the cat that was still in his view more interesting.

"Come on, I'll take you to the park...," Lisa began.

"Where you played as a child?" Peter finished.

"Hey cheeky, you love it there."

"Can we play football?"

"We'll have to call in at the newsagents on the way. I'm sure that they sell footballs in there."

Peter grabbed Lisa's hand and pulled her in the direction of the newsagents.

Derek, a tree surgeon, and his wife of many years, Sylvia, felt that they had settled into the Parkins old family home. His profession made them an honest living that enabled them both to maintain a comfortable lifestyle without her needing to go out to work; well, to do a conventional job anyway.

At local fairs and in private homes, Sylvia would read peoples palms or give tarot readings. It was a hobby that she enjoyed, and people paid her for the privilege. Although most of her customers were pleasant, she would, on occasion, meet some that would either pick fun at her or take it far too seriously.

On one particular occasion, an anxious customer was so obsessed with his death that he asked Sylvia for the exact date and time that he would take his last breath and what it was that would finish him off. She tried to explain, as calmly as possible, that she would not be able to do that. He jumped up. His chair fell back and crashed to the floor. He leant over the table and his face reddened. The veins on his temples bulged and looked like they might burst. He shouted obscenities and told her she was a fraud. With the palm of his hand in front of her face, he demanded a full refund. Confrontation was not her forte and the man was reimbursed before he was escorted from the premises.

Though to the other extreme, when a young couple mocked Sylvia, she decided to mix things up halfway through their reading. She wanted to teach the pair a lesson. Smiles were wiped off their faces when she pretended that she had gone into a trance during their sitting. She waited for them to stop with their stupidity and she snapped out of her daze. She apologised and told them that she had witnessed one of her visions. They did not appear often, but when they did, they were always vivid and accurate. At first, she claimed that she would not be able to divulge the predication with them, on account of it being against association regulations. The couple demanded that she tell them, as it was their right to know if it concerned them. Their persuasiveness caused her to give in, but she made them promise that they would not tell anyone where they had got the information from before she would reveal it to them. The couple agreed. She concocted a story and it flowed from her tongue. It was a tale that would haunt them for years and for the rest of their short lives. The mortified couple left. She felt no remorse.

Derek's profession was less eventful. He preferred the simpler way of life. Most days, he could be found cutting down a tree or two before either chopping them up into logs for firewood or putting them through a wood chipping machine. He would take regular breaks to enjoy his flask of tea and indulge in the odd chocolate biscuit.

It had taken a great deal of hard work to get the Moles' new home renovated from top to bottom. Much to Sylvia's dismay, the workmen had ambled in and out with their work boots on and dragged the dirt in with them daily. The interior of the house was transformed and as Derek and Sylvia wanted it. But there was still the overhaul of the back garden to sort.

Derek stood with his hands on his hips outside the back door of the house. Sylvia was by his side. They were looking into the garden at the mass of overgrowth. A mammoth job lay ahead of him and he felt exhausted thinking about it. He sighed out loud. "I'm going to have to make a start on this back garden at some point." He glanced at her. *I'm hoping that she'll volunteer to give me a hand.*

"Good luck with that. It'll make up for you not helping me when I spent every day cleaning up after those bloody workmen." Sylvia pointed at the outhouse. Its door was hanging off and was, by some small miracle, holding on by the top hinge. "We need to get that outside toilet knocked down. It's a right eyesore and it stinks. Think of the extra room we'll have in the garden." She put her arm around Derek's shoulders.

"We could put one of those man-caves there," Derek said. *I'd better get my idea in first before she says anything.* "Do you know the ones that I mean? They look quite similar to one of those summer houses that you were looking at in that catalogue." He turned his head to look at her. *I wonder what her answer will be.*

Sylvia did not react straight away as she had several ideas of her own. She replied with a smug expression, "Okay, you can have your man-cave, but... you have to landscape the rest of the garden and put a nice water feature in that corner." She pointed to the top left-hand side of the garden and wiggled her finger. *I know he'll agree because I'm letting him have that hide-out that he's hinted at for years.*

Derek smiled. *I knew what she was going to say before she even opened her mouth. I know her better than what she knows herself.* "Okay, it's a deal. Now get in that house and put the kettle on."

Sylvia moved her arm from Derek's shoulders and turned to walk into the house. Before he realised what he was doing, he had slapped her bottom. She grabbed his wrist and smacked the back of his hand. "Behave, Mr Mole." The two of them giggled as they walked inside the house and flicked each other's arms, like a couple of adolescents.

Derek was in the living room when Sylvia shouted through to him, "Did you lock the back door?"

"No and I'm guessing that you obviously didn't." Derek shook his head as he walked past Sylvia. The key was in the keyhole. He reached to turn it, but he stopped when he caught sight of what looked like a shadow outside. It appeared to be detached and had no actual body connected to it. It moved towards their garden. He needed to get a better look. He pressed his face against the door's glass panel, but whatever it was appeared to have gone. He presumed that it must have been the black tomcat that lived next door. Locking the door, he pulled the safety chain across.

Picking up the kettle, Sylvia checked on the water level. There was enough to make them both a drink, but she still filled it to its maximum mark. It was a habit that she did every time without thinking about it. She placed the kettle on the work surface and switched it on. The glowing blue light that was on its lid was mesmerising.

Derek was in the living room and rummaging through one of the drawers of the dresser. He managed to find a writing pad and pencil beneath a pile of brown envelopes. Sitting on the sofa, he began sketching an outline of what their back garden could look like. Sylvia joined him. She perched on the arm of the sofa and looked over his shoulder. She was impressed with his enthusiasm and watched with interest as he began by adding the water feature to the corner of his drawing. She heard the kettle as it switched itself off with a click. Pushing herself up, she made her way into the kitchen.

Sylvia was standing with her back to the kitchen window as she reached into the cupboard to grab a couple of mugs. The room darkened. *It became overcast quickly. There must be a storm on its way.* She turned to look out of the window. Screaming, she dropped the mugs. They fell, as though in slow motion, and shattered on the floor. There, hovering on the other side of the window pane was a black shadow. It was leaning forward and appeared to be watching her.

At first, the black shadow did not move, but disappeared seconds before Derek strolled into the kitchen with a rolled-up newspaper in his hand. The natural daylight returned. He had heard Sylvia's scream and the mugs smashing. "Where is it?" He presumed that it was a spider that was to blame and had come equipped to squash it. Rolling up his sleeves, he scoured the room for the little intruder.

Sylvia checked outside the window before she answered, "Where's what?" Her voice quivered as she spoke. *I can't believe he's going to try and hit whatever it was with a rolled-up newspaper. What good will that do?*

"The spider." Derek began moving items around on the work surface as he continued in his search. *I've lost count of how many creepy crawlies I've killed for her, over the years that we've been together.*

"What spider?" Sylvia joined Derek in his search.

"If it wasn't a spider, then what made you screech?" Derek put the newspaper onto the table and tried to flatten it.

"Oh, it's nothing... just me being daft. I thought that I saw something outside the window, and it made me jump... that's all." Sylvia looked pale and had a troubled expression. She opened the door beneath the kitchen sink, crouched and reached inside for the dustpan and brush. Picking up the larger broken pieces, with care, she swept up the smaller bits and emptied the dustpan into the kitchen bin.

"It was probably next door's cat. It's always skulking around and making a bloody nuisance of itself." Derek stroked her cheek with the backs of his fingers. *I'm just trying to reassure her, but whatever it was seems to have really startled her.* "I think I saw the pesky thing going up into our garden when I was locking the back door earlier."

Sylvia looked at Derek, but she did not respond. *I appreciate his concern, but I know that he'll never believe me.* She smiled and nodded as though she were in agreement. Reaching into the cupboard, she grabbed a couple more mugs.

Derek left Sylvia making the brews in the kitchen and made his way to the living room. He continued with his plan for the garden. *I know that something's not right and that she's not telling me everything. I'll give her some space so that she can think things over. Past experience has taught me, on more than one occasion that it's easier not to push her. She'll talk when she's ready.*

Sylvia tried to keep herself busy during the hours that followed but kept picturing the black shadow.

It was usual for Sylvia to call Derek through, but he was only aware that their evening meal was ready when he heard the clattering of the cutlery and crockery on the table. He had also smelt the spicy aromas that drifted into the living room.

Derek's concerns grew as they sat at the table to eat. *It usually only takes her an hour or two to confide in me, but still she hasn't said one word.* Sylvia stopped gawking at the television at random intervals to nibble at her food. It was not a deliberate act on her part, but more of a preoccupied type of silence.

When Derek and Sylvia had finished eating, he suggested that she might like to go and put her feet up in the living room whilst he cleared the table. She nodded in agreement. He scraped the leftovers into the waste food unit on the worktop and loaded the dirty cutlery and crockery into the dishwasher.

Derek was about to turn around, to check that he had cleared everything from the table, but he stopped himself when he sensed that he was no longer alone. It wasn't Sylvia. He knew that she was in the living room as he had looked through the doorway and he could hear her turning the pages of his newspaper. Something else was watching him. He turned around. His heart began to beat faster when he saw the black shadow hovering near the back door.

Despite Derek's heart pounding fast, he pretended that he had not seen the black shadow. *Just ignore it. Denial is always the easier option.* He placed the last dishwasher tablet into the machine and threw the empty box into the recycling bin. Pressing the 'economy setting' button, he closed its door. He listened as the water rushed in. It sloshed and hissed alongside the hum of the motor. *Admit it. It wasn't next door's cat that you saw wandering up into the garden. It was the same black shadow that you witnessed earlier and it's, more*

181

than likely, what Sylvia saw that's scared her half to death. He turned off the lights and television and joined Sylvia in the living room.

After switching on the wall lights and the table lamp, Derek turned his head to look through into the kitchen, but the soft light in the living room was too dim to cast any light into the far corner of the kitchen. *I hope that thing's gone.*

Derek was standing next to the door that led from the living room into the kitchen. His palms were perspiring as he waited for the black shadow to jump out at him. He did not dare to look into the kitchen as he pushed against the door handle. The door creaked before it clicked shut. *Why haven't I noticed the door making that noise before?* He felt certain that the black shadow was lurking on the other side as he stood there for a moment longer gripping the handle. *If it really wanted to get to us, then it isn't going to let a door stand in its way. It'll probably just pass through it, and me, for that matter.*

After drawing the curtains, Derek sat next to Sylvia on the sofa. The two of them were silent and his vacant and distant facial expression was a likeness to hers. He needed to talk to her about what he thought he had seen but pondered over how he might broach the subject without making her feel anxious. He decided not to mention it; nevertheless, he continued to listen for any unusual noises.

Derek leant forward and picked up the television guide magazine from the coffee table. There was a rugby match being aired and it was a game that he did not want to miss. He flicked through the pages until he was on the right day and checked down each channel's column to see what time the game was on. He looked at his wristwatch. "Sylvia, the rugby game's due to start in a few minutes. Do you mind if I put the telly on and watch it in here?" *Surely she'll say yes as the telly would already be on if there was something on that she'd wanted to watch.*

Sylvia looked at Derek. Her eyes were filled with tears. "No, I don't mind." But her tears and teeth biting into her lip would suggest that there was something wrong.

Throwing the magazine onto the coffee table, Derek picked up the television remote control and moved closer to Sylvia. He placed his hand on top of her knee. "Oh, whatever is the matter, Sylvia? Please tell me." He waited until she raised her eyes to look at him before he continued, "Does me watching the rugby really upset you that much?"

Derek's attempt at humour went unnoticed as Sylvia placed the newspaper on top of the magazine. "I need to tell you something, but I want you to promise me that you won't laugh. Just listen and try to believe me. I know that you're a sceptic, but I really need you to be a little bit more open-minded." She paused

183

because she was not going to tell him anything until he had given her his word.

"I promise." Derek planted a gentle kiss on Sylvia's forehead.

Sylvia gave Derek a stern look. "No, I mean… *really* promise me."

"I've given you my word, Sylvia. I want you to tell me what's bothering you. I'm listening. I'm pretty sure that we can work through whatever it is… together."

Sylvia exhaled audibly before she started to explain, "Well, remember earlier today when I squealed in the kitchen and you asked me what the matter was?" She began to study Derek's facial expression and gauged his reaction before she continued, "You thought I'd seen a spider and came to my rescue with a rolled-up newspaper in your hand."

"Yes," Derek answered. *I know that Sylvia's watching me. She'll be analysing my posture, the way I speak, how my lips move and where I look. If I make just one wrong move, she'll claim that I'm not really interested. I want her to continue. In fact, I need confirmation. Have we witnessed the same thing? I hope that we bloody well haven't.*

"You said that it was probably next door's cat." Sylvia gave Derek's knee a quick squeeze as though she was chastising him for not realising what the matter was.

Derek moved his hand from Sylvia's knee, rubbed the top of his knee and resisted the temptation to say 'ouch'. "I remember," he nodded in agreement. He wanted to show her that he was listening; however, not too much, to avoid the accusation of him being cynical.

"Well I know it wasn't next door's cat because whatever it was filled the entire window." Sylvia was standing in front of Derek and demonstrating the enormity of what she had seen by stretching out her arms. "I've absolutely no idea what it was. I've never seen anything like it before in my life. All I can tell you is that it was black and like an endless gloom with no obvious features, but it was in the shape of a human. I think!"

Yes, it certainly sounds like what I saw. "Okay." It was the only word that Derek could think of. *I know that I should really be saying more and acting a little bit more shocked, but I think I'll just keep my version of events to myself for the time being. I don't want Sylvia panicked any more than what she already is.*

"I knew you wouldn't believe me," Sylvia sighed as her shoulders and head slumped. *I knew that I was being too optimistic in expecting my husband to be even the slightest bit open-minded.*

Oh no, here we go. Derek patted the sofa cushion next to him as he urged Sylvia to sit beside him.

Sylvia took no notice of Derek's request and continued to stand. She was glaring at him as she waited for his response.

"I'm sorry, Sylvia. I was just keeping quiet so that you could get it all off your chest. I do believe you saw something, and I know you probably think that it's to do with the paranormal, but there's probably a perfectly logical scientific explanation." Derek could not believe the words that were coming out of his mouth. *You saw it for yourself. Why are you trying to deny it?*

Shaking her head, Sylvia reached to grab the remote control from Derek's hand. *I'm just wasting my breath.* She aimed it at the television and pressed a number of buttons. A couple of seconds later, the rugby game appeared on the screen with commentators stating the obvious. She slumped onto the sofa and stared at the television.

The atmosphere in the room was heavy as Derek sat and watched the game. *I can't seem to do right for doing wrong.*

Why can't Derek just be a little more understanding? He's such a stubborn old fool. Sylvia's eyelids felt heavy. She began to drop off to sleep, but her whole body went into a spasm and she woke with a start. Looking at Derek, she prodded his arm. "What was the name of that woman at Fred's retirement party? The one that was chain-smoking and claimed to be Beechwood's medium."

Derek turned and looked at Sylvia with a blank expression. Had he heard what she was asking him or was he trying to remember the woman's name? His attention wavered between Sylvia and the television before he said, "Do you mean Linda who works in the charity shop?"

Sylvia picked up the remote from her lap. It had fallen from her grip as she had begun to doze. She tapped Derek's knuckles with it. "Yes, that's her. I think I need to go and have a chat with Linda. I'll invite her around to the house. I need to get some advice and ask if she'd be interested in holding a séance, here, in our home."

"Sounds like a good idea," Derek agreed without hesitation. *I daren't disagree. It's more than my life's worth.* He reached for the newspaper, found the sudoku puzzle, folded the page and placed it on the coffee table. *I'll solve that one later once this rugby game's finished.*

A feeling of fresh optimism changed Sylvia's mood. *Now then, should I go and finish that bottle of wine that's in the fridge that was left over from last night?*

As Sylvia walked towards the kitchen, she stopped next to the door. Her hand was wrapped around the handle when she turned to look at Derek. "Would you like me to get you a glass of wine or a can of beer from the fridge? I'm going to get one for myself." The door creaked as she opened it.

Derek looked beyond her and into the kitchen. He did not appear to be listening and was focusing on the darkness that lurked behind her. *Should I warn her? How can I? I'd drop myself right in it and reveal what I've seen at the same time. Stop worrying, she'll be okay. If that black shadow was going to do something it would have done it by now. Besides, it's probably moved on.*

"Are you okay?" Sylvia reached through into the kitchen and felt about on the wall for the light switch. "Derek, do you want anything to drink?" The kitchen lit up.

"Not at the moment, thanks." Derek leant forward as Sylvia was standing in the doorway and blocking his view. "I might grab one for myself when the game is over."

Sylvia turned and looked into the kitchen. *What's wrong with him? What's he looking at?* "Derek, are you sure that you're all right?"

Derek's attention was back on the rugby game. "Yes, I'm fine," he said in a matter-of-fact manner. *Anyway, it looks like whatever it was has disappeared.*

Sylvia took the bottle from the fridge, got a glass from the cupboard, sat at the table and finished the wine. She looked over at the window. *I wonder if that black shadow is lurking to the other side of that blind.* She grabbed another bottle from the wine rack and under the influence of alcohol, it did not take long until her anxieties slipped from her mind and she thought of nothing.

The rugby match was over and had resulted in Derek's team losing. It left him feeling disappointed. He stayed in the living room and slouched on the sofa with his feet resting on the coffee table. *Too many missed opportunities and damn those linesmen and that flaming referee. They're all cheating bastards. It's fixed. We needed those points as well. I wish I hadn't bothered to watch it.* He picked up the newspaper and began trying to solve the sudoku puzzle, but it got the better of him when penned numbers started to get written over the top of each other and it became illegible. *I knew I should've used a pencil. Come on, get yourself up to bed.*

The lamp switch clicked as Derek reached over his bedside cabinet to turn it off. The sound amplified against the stillness of the night. He waited for a moment longer to make sure that it had not disturbed Sylvia. He wriggled in a downwards motion until his head was on the pillow and he pulled the duvet over his shoulders. He drifted off to sleep and began to snore.

With her back to Derek, Sylvia lay motionless. She was curled up on her side and suffering with the effects of the wine. Their bedroom seemed to be spinning. Listening to her stomach churn and to the rhythm of his snoring, she closed her eyes. She took deeper breaths to slow down her breathing and eventually fell asleep.

The next morning, Derek had showered, got dressed and made breakfast before Sylvia had managed to wake from her slumber or 'beauty sleep' as she often referred to it.

Sylvia woke and, at first, she did not move. The smell of burnt toast filled the house. *What time is it? Hang on a minute, what day is it?* She began to rise. Her lips felt dry as she ran her tongue over them, and her right eyelid was refusing to open. She scratched her

189

head as she swung her legs over the side of the bed. Sliding her feet along the carpet, she searched for her slippers. Without warning, her eyelid decided to open. She looked at the floor. Her vision was blurry as she shuffled her feet into her slippers. She felt dizzy as she stood up. She felt her way along the wall until she reached her dressing gown and removed it from one of the hooks behind the door. Her head was pounding. It was one of those pulsating headaches that is always accompanied with a feeling of nausea. Making her way to the top of the stairs, she caught sight of herself in the full-length mirror on the landing. Her hair was sticking to one side of her face whilst on the other side, it stuck out. She had bags underneath her bloodshot eyes and swollen eyelids. *Are my lips blue?* Creases lay on her face in random places and stood out against her flushed skin.

After making her way to the top of the stairs, Sylvia shuffled down on her bottom and into the kitchen in an unladylike manner, tackling each stair individually. As she got halfway, she could hear the fizzing sound of Alka Seltzer. Derek had heard her creaking around upstairs and started to get the hangover cure ready. He found it comical as she walked towards him with her shoulders and head slumped as though it was too heavy for the body carrying it; however, he did not show his amusement.

Derek had set two places at the table with fresh orange juice, freshly ground coffee and a round of toast.

For a moment, he had considered making a full English breakfast, but remembered the outcome from the last hangover and decided to keep it simple.

Pulling out Sylvia's chair, Derek gestured for her to sit and whispered, "Good morning, my love, and how are you feeling today?" *I think I already know what the answer to that one will be.* He held the back of her chair and steadied her as she lowered herself onto it.

Sylvia picked up the glass of Alka Seltzer, placed its rim against her bottom lip and opened her mouth several millimetres. She tipped her head back and began to sip. Its bubbles hit her in the face. She was not enamoured with the taste but knew that it would help. She gulped it down. Its fizziness shot up her nose. "Well I've felt...," a belch stopped her mid-sentence, "whoops, excuse me... I've felt better, Derek." She propped her elbows on the table and rested her forehead against her fingertips. "Why ever did you let me finish that second bottle?"

Derek poured himself another coffee, turned and looked at Sylvia. She had not moved. "Do you want a coffee or anything, love?" He felt the urge to laugh but didn't.

"Not at the moment," Sylvia answered. "I just need to give myself a little bit more time to recover and then I'll see how I feel."

"Okay." Derek pressed his foot on the pedal of the kitchen bin. Its lid sprung open. He tipped Sylvia's plate onto its side and watched as the toast fell in.

"I just don't understand why I feel so bad this morning," Sylvia mumbled. "I can usually drink that amount of alcohol, no problem." She turned her head to one side and her eyes followed as she tried to locate Derek. "I must be under the weather."

"Yes, that's probably it." Derek recalled Sylvia having a hangover a couple of weeks earlier and her saying the same thing.

"I'm going to go into the village today to see if that Linda is working in the charity shop. I need to have a chat with her about what you and I discussed last night." Sylvia lifted her head.

Derek looked into the corner of the kitchen where he had seen the black shadow the previous night. There wasn't anything to see, but that did not stop him from feeling uneasy. *Perhaps it's close by and listening to our every word and watching our every move.* "If that's what you want love." He smiled. "Do I really need to be here when you have that séance though?"

"No... not if you don't want to be." Sylvia pushed her empty glass to one side, folded her arms and put them on the table. "I know you don't believe in any of that mumbo jumbo, as you call it, so I won't force you." She rested her head on her arms and closed her eyes.

Chapter Twelve
The Séance

Waste bags and gardening tools were lined up next to Derek. He was ready to do battle with the back garden and would start by clearing the overgrowth. With his arms folded, he stared at the garden. He tried to picture what it would look like once it was finished, but he could only imagine those twinges in his lower back.

A séance was about to begin in the kitchen. Starting on the garden seemed like the perfect excuse to avoid getting drawn into it all.

Several days had gone by since Sylvia had met up with Linda for that chat and Linda had said she was more than happy to help. She had invited along two of her acquaintances. Larry Hennessay was a tall, rotund silver-haired gentleman who was also a medium. His partner June Pennock, who was a petite lady, had accompanied him. She did not have any psychic abilities but was fascinated by anything to do with the paranormal.

After introductions had been made and refreshments served, Linda asked Sylvia, Larry and June to take their seats around the table. Linda continued to stand, reached into her handbag and pulled out a box of matches. She struck one of them and lit the candle that was in a tall silver candlestick in the middle of the table. The smell of sulphur from the spent match filled the room. She moved towards the window, paused for a moment and looked out at Derek in the garden before closing the blind.

The four of them sat in silence as they waited for the flame to still.

Sylvia was hesitant as she looked at the other three in turn. *I don't really know these people that are sitting in my kitchen, staring at a flame and are about to attempt to make contact with someone or something from the other side. What the hell was I thinking? Nothing strange has happened for days. Maybe it was just a one-off. Should I just call the whole thing off?*

It was too late. The séance had begun. Larry was sitting upright with his eyes closed. His palms were flat against the tablecloth and his fingers were spread. Linda, who was sitting opposite him, imitated his actions. Sylvia was not sure if she should be doing the same and looked over at June who was sitting with her arms folded, eyes wide and staring with a vacant expression at nothing in particular. Aware that Sylvia was watching her, June glanced at her before she leant forward and copied Larry while she made sure that her little fingers were touching his and Linda's. Sylvia followed suit.

There was an eerie silence. Sylvia had started to feel awkward. The séance was not what she had expected and quite a bit different from how they portrayed such things in the movies. *Isn't someone supposed to say something so that the other side knows that we're trying to make contact?*

An icy-cold draught passed behind Sylvia. She was sure that something had touched her with its fingertips and stroked the back of her neck. Her hairs were standing on end and her body was rigid. She opened her eyes and tried to catch sight of whatever it was, but there did not appear to be anything there. *Is that black shadow that I saw outside the kitchen window now inside my home?* Linda and Larry remained calm with their eyes closed and though June's eyes were shut, she somehow continued with that oblivious facial expression. *Am I the only one that's noticed that we're no longer alone?*

The temperature in the room dropped further. Sylvia noticed the thin clouds of vapour in front of each of their faces as they exhaled. The candles flame flickered before it lay horizontal and blew out. The room darkened. Small shafts of light filtered around the edges of the blind and through the glass in the back door.

Linda gasped and revealed the whites of her knuckles as she gripped the edge of the table. She pulled on its tablecloth and caused the candlestick to wobble. It fell and the thud echoed as though it were in a vast empty room.

June flinched and opened her eyes.

"I feel a presence here with us in this room," Linda began as she placed her palms onto the table. "Whatever happens we must remain calm and show no fear."

Sylvia was not sure if she was supposed to laugh or cry. *Show no fear? What the hell? Linda certainly isn't following her own rules.*

Larry remained quiet throughout, but the hairs standing proud on his arms confirmed that he had also felt a presence.

Serenity resumed; however, it was to be short-lived.

Gasping, as though surprised, Larry opened his eyes wide before they rolled back inside their sockets until only the bloodshot white was visible.

"Who are you?" Linda was trying to communicate with whatever was trying to channel itself through Larry. Her face grew paler with darkened eye sockets and looked similar to his.

No response was given from either Larry or the spirit. He began to fidget on his seat. The room was cold and yet numerous sweat beads had formed across his forehead.

Linda began to question him, but this time her approach was firmer, "I asked you a question. Tell me who you are!"

"You already know who I am," Larry responded with the spirit's voice. His pupils became visible again as he returned Linda's stare.

June felt about inside one of her pockets and pulled out a screwed-up tissue. She was not sure if she had used it or not; nevertheless, she leant forward and began to wipe Larry's brow. But, when her fingertips touched him, she was met with an electric shock. It travelled with speed up her arm and the pain finished in her armpit. Rubbing her arm, she stumbled back onto her seat.

"No, you're mistaken. That's why I asked you the question? Are you able to give me your name?" Linda's palms felt clammy and the tightness in her chest was making it harder for her to breathe. "Do I need to make any introductions or are you already aware of who we all are?"

Sylvia noticed a strange odour. It was comparable to decaying meat and it made her cough. She found it hard to stop as her face reddened and her eyes streamed. She looked at each of the others, in turn, whilst she pulled herself together, but the others continued with the séance. *I don't even think any of them have noticed that smell or me almost choking to death.* The front of her head was pounding, and she could feel that her heart was beating faster.

"Hello, John Parkins," Larry said. A droplet of blood emerged from the end of his nose. He seemed unaware of it as it lengthened and then fell onto the tablecloth. He was not able to move, and it was only going to be a matter of time until he would be drained of energy.

"It's time to put a stop to all of this, Peter Hurst," Linda wheezed as she glared at Larry.

June looked at Sylvia with an expression of disbelief. She had never witnessed Larry and Linda being channelled at the same time and they were having a conversation. Neither June nor Sylvia spoke. They were scared that something detrimental may happen if they did.

"You may refer to me as Peter, if you so wish, but I have no one specific name. I have no name, yet I have been called many things. A name would be of no use to me; however, I am many souls who once had names, but they are no longer of any relevance to either me or you." The whites of Larry's eyes began to turn red as they filled with blood. "What is it that I need to put a stop to? Weren't you the one that was involved with drugging Peter until he was unable to move? And then did you not stab him repeatedly, which, correct me if I am wrong, makes you in line with a demon also?"

"You got your revenge and now it's time for you to move on from this realm," Linda implored. Her breathing had eased, but she looked like she might collapse at any moment.

Larry let out a raucous laugh which stopped when he began to cough and splutter. He was out of his trance, but his nose bled a steady stream and it trickled down in equal measures from both of his nostrils. Nosebleeds for him at séances were common, but this one was heavier than usual and had come on earlier in the proceedings.

He put his hand up to tackle the blood flow and pinched his nose.

Grabbing the kitchen roll from the side, June tore off several sheets and folded them along the perforations. She moved to Larry's side, put her hand on the back of his head and coerced him into putting his head forward while she passed the sheets to him.

"Find, Lisa," Linda shouted. "She's the only one that can stop that black shadow from killing anyone else."

June looked at Sylvia and asked, "Who's Lisa?"

"I'm almost sure that was the name of one of the daughters that used to live here before we bought the house," Sylvia responded.

"Lisa needs to move his remains. She knows where they are." Linda pointed towards the back garden. "She needs to get rid of that tree, chop it down and destroy its roots. There needs to be no trace of it left behind. That thing needs to be stopped before it takes any more souls." Her shoulders slumped as she folded her arms. Placing them on the table, she rested her head.

Sylvia looked confused. *Move whose remains and destroy what tree? There isn't a tree in my back garden. Hopefully, Linda's mistaken about the body as well.*

Larry's nose had stopped bleeding; however, he was preoccupied with prodding the index finger of his left hand up each of his nostrils, in turn, to make sure.

Getting to her feet, Sylvia walked towards the back door. She unlocked it and opened it to allow the natural daylight in. The mild fresh air drifted through and started to rid the kitchen of that smell of death. She rolled up the blind and the light shone through. Reaching for the kettle, she topped it with water and flicked on its switch. She looked around her kitchen and asked, "Anyone for refreshments?"

No-one answered.

June strolled towards the back door and leant against its frame. She looked into the garden. Breathing in the fresh air, she turned to look at Sylvia and said, "It appears that somebody by the name of Lisa needs to move a body that's buried in your back garden."

June's comment made Sylvia feel anxious. *I wish she'd keep her voice down. What if Derek or one of my neighbours has heard what she's just said? How am I supposed to explain all of this to Derek? He's going to dig over the garden and find the body anyway. I suppose I'd better tell him sooner rather than later.* Sylvia turned to look at Linda as she needed her advice, but she was sleeping. There was drool trickling down from the corner of her open mouth. Sylvia turned to ask Larry, "Do you think that I should call the police?"

The whites of Larry's eyes were no longer filled with blood, but they were still bloodshot. He stood and walked towards Sylvia. He was unsteady on his feet and looked like his legs might give way. Placing his hands on the kitchen work surface, he propped himself up and looked out of the kitchen window. He moved closer to Sylvia to give her his opinion. "That would have to be your decision, but if you do decide to go to the police then you'll need to explain to them how you knew where the body was? I doubt they would believe that a spirit at a séance told you." He saw that Derek was gardening. "Although, it might be a good idea to warn your husband. If he does come across the body, then it won't come as such a shock to him. He could tell the police that he found it when he was digging the garden over. Remember, whatever was said at this séance today remains totally confidential. Not one of us will say a word to anyone else outside of this room." He paused before continuing as though an afterthought had popped into his head. "There is something else that you might like to consider. It's been known that sometimes a few spirits like to be the jokers. Just because they've passed over to the other side it doesn't mean that they've lost their sense of humour. It could be possible that they are simply having a bit of fun with us."

Sylvia felt nervous as she chuckled. "I'll need to give it some thought, but I don't think I'll mention anything to Derek, not just yet, anyway." Turning around, she looked at Linda. "Is she going to be okay?" She bit against her lip.

"Oh yes, Linda will be fine. Just give her a few minutes and she'll bounce back as though nothing's happened. She'll soon be back to her usual self and reaching for her cigarettes," Larry said.

"Excuse me," Derek said as he squeezed past June in the doorway. He stood on the doormat with his soiled boots on and looked at Sylvia. It was hard for him to ignore the strange smell that lingered and that the ambience in the room felt heavy. "Everything okay, love?" He sniffled and wiped his nose with the back of his hand. He had noticed the blood on the tablecloth and gave a disapproving look.

Sylvia nodded. "Yes, fine." She continued to look into the garden.

I'd say that her two-word answer is a sure sign that something's not okay. "That's good to hear. I'm just going to take a break. Is there any chance of you making me a strong coffee?" Derek held up his grass stained hands to show Sylvia. "I'll take it outside with me."

"I'm on it," Sylvia answered.

Sylvia's hands are shaking. Oh no... she's going to burst into tears, and I can't get over to her, to comfort her, without leaving behind a trail of dirt. Derek tried to distract the attention away from her. "Is Linda okay?" he asked Larry. "It looks like she's having a bit of a snooze."

"She's absolutely fine," Larry replied as though he was addressing an outsider.

Derek looked at each of them, in turn. *What the hell's been going on inside my house? I wonder if any of these so-called psychics can read what's on my mind.*

"Linda, like me, is what's known as a vessel. Souls that have passed over to the other side are able to use our bodies and absorb our energies in order to be able to communicate with the living," Larry said. However, he knew that his explanation was falling on a sceptic's ears as he had encountered Derek's type many times before.

Deciding it more polite not to respond, Derek chose to smile at Larry. *He's a pompous arse! Something's clearly troubling my Sylvia, though. I'll get them all to leave. Wait... no, I'd better not. I don't want to embarrass my wife by being rude to her guests.*

Linda began to murmur as she stirred from her nap. She lifted her head and ran the tip of her tongue over her smarting lips. "What the hell's just happened?" Her pale skin emphasised her bloodshot eyes while that overpowering smell appeared to ooze from her pores. Sylvia noticed that Larry smelt similar. "I feel like I've just run a marathon." She gasped for breath as she rubbed her aching muscles. She tried to stand, but Larry had to rush over to help her. "Would you and June mind driving me home?" she asked Larry. "I really don't feel well and all I want to do is go home to my bed."

June collected all of their personal belongings. Derek stepped outside the back door and moved to one side to allow Linda, Larry and June to pass. The three of them left without looking back or bothering to say goodbye to Sylvia.

Keeping quiet, Derek watched as the three of them left. *Good riddance.* He took off his boots and left them outside the back door. After washing his hands at the kitchen sink, he joined Sylvia at the table. He looked her in the eye. *How can I deny what's staring me right in the face and probably has been since the day that we moved in?* "We're not alone, are we, Sylvia? There's something else living in our house with us."

Sylvia leant forward and put her hand onto the top of his thigh. *He believes me.* She smiled.

"What are we supposed to do now?"

"I don't know." Sylvia shrugged.

The two of them sat in silence until they were interrupted by the sound of someone's persistent knocking on their front door. "I'll go," Derek said. "One of them has probably forgotten something." *Like their bloody manners and I don't want them upsetting Sylvia again.*

Sylvia could not make out what Derek and their caller were saying. Their conversation sounded muffled. She stood and walked through to join them.

There was a young woman standing at their front door. She was holding a little boy's hand. Derek turned to look at Sylvia and said, "This is, Lisa, and her son, Peter. She used to live here and was just in the neighbourhood. She was wondering if it would be possible for them both to come in and have a look at what we've done to the place."

Unable to move, Sylvia stared wide-eyed at Lisa and said nothing. Her legs weakened and she felt like she might vomit.

Peter smiled at Sylvia whilst Lisa gave her a wave and said, "Hi."

Sylvia began to shake her head and said, "No." She turned and made her way to the kitchen, as she needed to sit.

Surprised by Sylvia's reaction, Derek said, "I'm sorry, Lisa, but you've just caught us at a bad time. Maybe another day." And with that, he shut the door.

Chapter Thirteen
The Lonely Drinker

If the weather allowed, Elizabeth would often find herself sitting at the bottom of the garden during the day or in the conservatory of an evening. On the pleasant days, she would watch as the lake cruise boats sailed by with excited families on board and on most occasions at least one of the passengers would wave. It would be a parent or grandparent and they would encourage the children to copy and behave as though they had been lost at sea for days and she was their first sign of life.

Feeling that she should know the captain of each boat by name, Elizabeth had seen them often and wondered if they had ever noticed her. Maybe, one day, the crew would mention her to the tourists as they showed them around the sights of the lake and announce her as 'Mrs Caplin, the beloved wife of a local property mogul'.

The adventurous tourists would hire boats for themselves. There were wooden rowing boats and canoes, small motorboats with flat bottoms and outboard engines, and an array of orange life jackets. Elizabeth noted that chivalry in the younger men did not exist as they allowed the women to row or steer whilst they struggled to keep their children seated. The men would sit back and not help in any way, as though they were strangers.

The people that were on board the larger private boats would make the most of their free time away from their everyday lives. They would take it in turn to water-ski and show off, as though they were putting on a performance for the cheering crowds. Their spectacular face plants made for comical entertainment.

Each morning there would be various groups of club swimmers who would take to the water before it got busy with the sporting activities. The days when there were grey clouds looming overhead would not deter them. Some would dress in wetsuits whilst others wore swimwear, as though they were going to spend the day at the beach. Elizabeth had decided that she would give it a go one day and take the plunge. It would be a real test of her character in such appealing, yet cold, waters. If she liked it, she might make it a regular pastime and if she did not, she would sit on the jetty and dip her toes into the water on the hot days.

Elizabeth would often sit alone and become lightheaded from the effects of the alcohol. She would forget about the tourists as she became hypnotised by the glistening clear water. The sunlight, sky and surrounding landscape would reflect off the water's surface and remain still in places until it was disturbed.

The days where Elizabeth would overlook dinner were becoming more frequent. Sometimes it was because she was not hungry and on other occasions it was because she could not be bothered to ask Eliza to fix her something to eat.

Across to Elizabeth's right, in the distance, was breath-taking scenery that was yet to be spoilt by man. She was surrounded by hills that were photographed hundreds of times each day. The duller days saw low-lying clouds that covered the tops of the hills whilst the mist hovered over the lake and gave it a hint of mystery. It was easy to feel calm in such a setting, yet she often felt alone.

Over to the left side of the lake were a few shops. One of them sold souvenirs and another your everyday groceries. The staff were kept busy with children who pestered their parents to buy them souvenirs that will be thrown into a drawer once they get home, to be forgotten.

A coffee shop, which was located next to the shops was popular with both tourists and the locals. Local sourced ice creams were available. Their delicious blueberry scones were a speciality and always made fresh on the premises each day. A covered seating area was situated outside where the adults sat and enjoyed their coffee whilst the youngsters fed the birds.

The swans would wade in to scare the smaller birds and steal their share of the food. When the larger birds have finished feeding, the smaller birds appear and scavenge for the leftovers. The pieces that are decaying and have sunk to the bottom of the lake are eaten by the fish.

Elizabeth was delighted that her grandson was staying with her for the weekend. She greeted Lisa and Peter at the double gates at the bottom of her drive. It was an obtrusive metal barrier which required security clearance before anyone was allowed to pass.

Lisa waited in her car. The gates began to open. *This gate's strange! What's the point of it? Any intruder can easily gain access to the property via the lake if they really wanted to.* Acknowledging Elizabeth with a wave, she drove past her and towards the outbuildings. The sound of loose chippings crunched beneath her tyres and some hit the underside of her car. Peter unfastened his seat belt, knelt on the seat and waved with excitement at his grandmother through the rear window.

Lisa was surprised to see that Susan's car was parked outside one of the outbuildings. *Mum never warned me that she'd be here.*

Peter jumped out of the car and left his door open. He ran to meet Elizabeth who was strolling up the drive. The gate was closing behind her. Lisa pulled his overnight case from the boot of her car, closed the doors and waited for them to join her.

Following Elizabeth inside the house, Lisa put Peter's case at the bottom of the stairs. Eliza would carry it up to his room when she had finished with her usual chores.

Lisa noted that the silver-framed wedding photograph of Robert and his late wife, Diane, was to the centre of the mantel over the fireplace in the living room. *It's remarkable how alike Diane and Mum are.* There was a wedding photograph of Robert and Elizabeth, a family picture of Susan, Karl, Stacey and Jane, and separate school pictures of both of the girls, but nothing of either Lisa or Peter. *Charming! I've given her plenty of photographs of us in the past as well.*

Elizabeth was sure that she had seen Diane's facial expression change into a scowl with narrowing eyes, on a number of occasions, as she walked around what was once her home. She looked forward to the day that Robert felt that he was able to put the picture somewhere out of her sight for safekeeping, like the bottom of the bin.

Elizabeth, Lisa and Peter strolled through the house and back outside into the garden. It was immaculate. The lawn had an incline. At the bottom there was a paved patio area where there was an assortment of rattan furniture and parasols to keep off the midday sun. There were roses running down to the left and right of the lawn. Each bush was pruned and supported with a stake that showed its name. Every plant grew blooms of different colours and varying shades and there was a large weeping willow tree that grew in the middle and sloped off to one side.

A boat, nothing too grand, was tied to Robert's private jetty. It would bob up and down on the water at the bottom of the garden. He would use it to entertain both new and existing clients with a tour around the lake whilst they sipped wine and dined on fine cuisine. Elizabeth was forced to look at his boat with the name 'Diane' in large black lettering painted on its side; yet another stark reminder of his past, which stared her in the face every day.

Lisa could see the back of Susan's head as she sat at the bottom of the garden looking out over the lake. She had not seen her since that day when she caught her locking lips with her ex. *Right, don't mention Bill to her or rise to her bait if she starts goading you. It's not the right time or place and especially not in front of Peter. I just need a little bit more time to think. I'll broach the subject with her later when it's just the two of us.* She was not in the right frame of mind to face her. *I think I'll just make my excuses and leave.*

"Come here, Peter, and give me a cuddle before I get going." Lisa crouched and Peter put his arms around her neck. "I'll pick you up on Sunday. Now, have a good time and be a good boy for your grandma."

"I will." Peter smiled. "You too, Mummy."

"You're not going already are you, Lisa? Our Susan's here." Elizabeth pointed towards the lake. "Aren't you going to say hello?"

Bloody hell, has my mother been drinking already? It's still early in the day. I can smell alcohol on her breath. Did she pour it over her flaming cereal? Lisa looked towards Susan and noticed her waving.

Lisa waved, but her facial expression remained serious. She turned to Elizabeth and said, "I'll stay a little longer on Sunday, if that's okay?"

"Bye, Mummy, love you," shouted Peter as he ran down the lawn towards his Auntie Susan.

Lisa watched as Peter ran into Susan's arms.

"You could sit and have a bit of dinner with us on Sunday, if you're not too late, Lisa," Elizabeth smiled and nodded as though answering for her. She knew that something was troubling Lisa. It was difficult to ignore the tension that was in the air. *Maybe she'll tell me over dinner.*

"That sounds like a plan and thanks again for looking after Peter. I really need a couple of nights to myself." Lisa walked inside the house. "See you, Mum, and please don't spoil him!"

"I'll try not to," Elizabeth chuckled as she walked down the garden to join Susan and Peter.

Lisa had not quite made it to the door when she caught sight of the black shadow as it descended the staircase. Without saying a word, she stopped and watched it hover for a short while before she continued on her way.

Chapter Fourteen
Paranormal Pandora

The entertainment was due to start at seven thirty. It had stated that time, in large black print, at the bottom of the advertising poster. Lisa looked at the clock on the far wall. It read 8.10 p.m. *Am I the only person in this room who's noticed that Paranormal Pandora is actually late? I've paid for this. Why isn't anyone bothering to tell us what's happening?*

Lisa was slumped on a seat to the centre of the back row with her right leg resting over the top of her left knee. Her arms were folded in an unapproachable manner. She was dressed, as usual, in jeans, tee shirt and trainers with tied laces that were too long and hung loose. She felt a little underdressed as she looked around the room and noticed what some of the others were wearing. They had made an effort as though dressing up for a night out. There was even the odd suit and tie on show.

The guests had purchased their drinks from the hotel bar. They were being served in some sort of flimsy plastic tumblers. *Perhaps the management and bar staff think that we're going to riot and there'll be a blood bath if we drink out of real glasses.* Finishing her pint,

Lisa put the empty tumbler underneath her chair and decided to leave it at that. If she had any more alcohol, then anything was possible; however, she did feel the urge to get tipsy, but also knew that she needed to keep a level head.

The sound of general chatter and occasional bursts of laughter could be heard coming from one lady who was sitting at the front. To pass the time, Lisa found herself listening in on other people's conversations and she tried to lip-read those that were sitting further away.

The hotel staff had made some sort of an attempt at decorating around the edges of the temporary stage with silver tasselled bunting. It looked like it was straight out of a packet and gave the appearance of something from a children's television programme or party, rather than for a supposedly serious adult gathering.

The blinds were closed behind Lisa and the lights lowered by way of a dimmer switch that was positioned next to the fire exit. An illuminated sign above its door spoilt the ambience.

A white plastic garden table and chair, which looked too uncomfortable to sit on, had been placed near to the back of the stage behind a microphone stand. To make the room appear more mystical one of those fog contraptions that emits clouds of vapour was placed in the front right corner of the stage and was working, at random, into the faces of the couple that were sitting in front of it. Nevertheless, the couple remained seated and would just cough and blink more when it went into action. Lisa watched them with intrigue and shook her head. *Why don't they just move seats?*

Lisa recognised that there were a few local people from Beechwood in attendance. Ben Cooper and Amanda Styles were sitting a couple of rows in front of her. She had seen them walk in together and watched them as they sat down. They had not looked over at her and if they had it was doubtful that they would even know who she was. *They're both wearing wedding bands. I presume that they're married to each other, but I'm surprised that Mr & Mrs Cooper are even still together because, from what I remember, they had a turbulent relationship. Anyway, aren't they a little faint-hearted for this type of event? The last time I saw them two was when they were running away from the scene of their supposed friend, Vicky's, murder.* She mused that neither of them had changed a great deal in appearance; however, they appeared quieter, more grown-up in their attitude and at least she was not giggling. Amanda looked to be in the later stages of pregnancy and looked restless as she wriggled about on her seat. Ben's hand was rested over hers as he kept looking and smiling at her. *I wonder why they're here. Are they going to try and communicate with Vicky? Apologise to her, perhaps?*

Lisa's eyes were drawn to a man that was seated in a wheelchair to the front of the room. At first, she was not able to place him.

His name was Martyn. Several years earlier he used to hang around in a gang with some other reprobates at Beechwood Park. He had been a heroin addict from a young age. His mother would take it in front of him and he would watch as she regularly overdosed. It was always down to him to ring for an ambulance. He knew the routine and the paramedics knew him by name. It was strange that Social Services never took him into care, but there were always plenty of 'uncles' to look out for him. He had never had a fatherly figure to look up to and show him a good way through life. At the time, he thought it was normal behaviour and that life was like that for everyone. By the time he found out that it wasn't, it was too late for him. He was bound to a wheelchair and had just had his remaining leg amputated, but it did not stop him from pumping more of the same shit into his veins. His hair, what was left of it, had large patches of alopecia. His torso and arms were skeletal and winding veins lay on top of his bones with open and picked sores to his elbows. His skin looked delicate as though it might tear if you touched it. On one arm, he had a large purple bruise that looked like it might take a while to fade. His eyes appeared soulless and distant as though nothing was going on behind them.

It was not until Martyn stretched his arms above him that Lisa saw the track marks. They were clearly visible and ran along the surface of his veins. The scars stood out like they were tattooed on his skin. It prompted a memory. He was the one with the blood trickling down his forearm, that evening in Beechwood Park, when she was making her way home before it got dark. *He's aged a lot faster than the years he's lived.* She knew for certain that it was him. *Why would someone commit themselves to such a slow painful suicide? Maybe he wanted to give up the drugs and he's tried to get help, but his addiction has taken hold of him like a vice.* He looked pitiful as he sat alone. He was desperate to get word from his mother and find out if she was at peace.

Mrs Blake, the local gossip who ran the village newsagents, was sitting in the row behind Martyn. She was perched in an unladylike manner. Leaning forward, she was not able to sit with her legs together and her hips and bottom hung over the sides of her seat. It looked possible that the seat might disappear if she sat on it for too long. To her side sat a slimmer man. *I wonder if that's her husband. No, he can't be. He looks too young, but anything's possible.* It looked like he had been dragged along to the event and had left his enthusiasm at home. *It's more likely that he's her son. Does she even have a man in her life or any offspring? Perhaps, he's a nephew?* Lisa did not know anything about her. She had never engaged in a conversation with her when she had gone into the newsagents and would always put what she needed onto the counter, give the daily pleasantries and hand over her money without making eye contact.

Derek and Sylvia were sitting to the centre of the front row. Lisa recognised them both when she saw them and after making the necessary enquiries, she now knew what their names were. For a moment, she considered reintroducing herself. *I think that's Linda sitting to the side of Derek, but I don't know who the other two are that are next to Sylvia. I've never seen them before.* Linda was leaning in front of Derek and chatting with Sylvia, Larry and June. They had their drinks in their hands and were eager for the show to start. Derek was the exception. He did not want to be there and had hoped that he had seen the last of the other three following that séance in his home, but Sylvia had heard about the event and decided that she wanted to make contact with them.

The seats were filling up, but the ones to either side of Lisa remained empty until an elderly gentleman appeared to the left of her. She did not see him take his seat and had no recollection of him disrupting the others on her row. Thinking him slightly odd, he made no attempts to speak or look at her. *He looks familiar, but it can't be who I'm thinking of. He looks like that priest that sheltered from the storm when I was having coffee with Bill, but what would he be doing in Beechwood? Hang on… didn't I see him in my hotel room as well? Maybe, he's got a doppelganger.*

The door at the front swung open. It was Mel. She had a red and blotchy face and looked like she had run all the way there. Lisa looked around the room and noticed that there were a small number of seats that were free. *I bet she just has to choose the one that's right next to me.* Mel brushed past the knees of the people that were sitting on the back row and stood to the side of Lisa. She took off her jacket, placed it over the back of her seat, looked at Lisa and smiled.

Lisa suddenly felt self-conscious as she returned Mel's smile. *I wonder if she knows that I watched as her daughter was murdered that day.* She was starting to feel uncomfortable. *Shit! Why didn't I think of that before? Some of these people want to make contact with spirits from the other side. What if they find out that some of their loved ones died because of me?* She began to fidget on her seat. *Perhaps, it's time for me to leave.*

"Oh, hi, Damian," Mel said to the elderly gentleman. "I nearly didn't recognise you wearing your civilian clothes. It was lovely to meet you at the train station. It's been a while. Perhaps, if you're not too busy, we could have a catch up later?"

Damian smiled and nodded.

Civilian clothes? It is that priest. I knew it was him. Lisa decided to stay. *I doubt anything will happen. Anyway, it'll look a bit odd if I just get up and leave and I've paid for the ticket. Should I swap seats with one of these two though?* She remained seated as Paranormal Pandora, the star of the show, had decided to put in an appearance.

Lisa noticed that Pandora had found the time to purchase a bottle of red wine from the bar, en route, as

219

she clambered up a step stool to get onto the stage. She balanced herself as she held the neck of the bottle in one hand and the stem of the wine glass in the other. The cork had already been removed from the bottle. For her size, her footsteps were light as she walked across the stage towards the chair. She placed the glass onto the table, with care, and poured herself a drink. She filled her glass to the rim.

A middle-aged lady with a fuller figure stood to the centre of the stage. Pandora's short black dyed hair stood out against her skin and highlighted a paler complexion. With over-plucked eyebrows, which gave her an expression of permanent surprise, she looked out at her audience. Smiling at everyone, but no one in particular, she appeared pleasant and had an evident abundance of stage confidence. She was dressed in a royal blue tailored trouser suit and her coordinating kitten heels looked tight as they dug into her skin. Red sores were present on her feet where blisters would follow.

Pandora's first words were an utterance at some kind of feeble apology. She had lost track of the time but did promise them a night to remember as she could feel a presence around them and without having to summon it.

Lisa was neither impressed nor convinced. *If this Paranormal Pandora is psychic, then I'm Marilyn Monroe.* It felt strange for her to be attending the event by herself as she was used to Peter being with her. They went everywhere together, but children were not allowed to attend for obvious reasons; although looking at the stage and at Pandora, she wondered if he might have found it all amusing.

Pandora's audience had started to settle as she leant forward to take a sip of her wine. She greeted the glass with puckered lips and left a bright red lipstick smudge on its rim. Standing upright, she swayed and licked her lips with an expression that would suggest that the taste was to her satisfaction. It was questionable if that was her first drink of the night.

The stage was set, and Paranormal Pandora's audience was ready to embrace her messages from beyond the grave. "Good evening, everyone, and thank you for joining me," she announced with a voice that was as loud as you would have imagined.

Random voices could be heard responding, "Good evening," and, "You're welcome." While the more daring shouted, "Just get on with it."

There was a pleasant aroma in the room. Lisa had been trying to work out what it was. It was a combination of smells that lingered from that evening's meals. It made her feel hungry. *I'll grab a bag of salted peanuts from the bar when the show's finished.*

Pandora waited until the room had quietened. "Again, I would like to apologise for being late." She smiled at the lady who was seated next to June on the front row. "I think that it's time to get started as there are a number of spirits with us this evening and they're eager to communicate with some of you." She looked at that same lady and nodded as though confirming what she had said.

Lisa looked around the room. All the seats were full. Her attention was drawn to a small flash of light that travelled with speed. She turned to see what it was and saw two orbs hovering motionless in the corner of the ceiling. Feeling a presence behind her, she turned to look who it was and noticed that a black shadow appeared to be sitting on one of the dining tables that had been pushed up against the wall underneath the window. Smiling, she turned to look at Pandora and caught Damian glancing at her.

Pandora's eyes widened as she stared at what was sitting behind Lisa.

Maybe, Pandora is the real deal after all, Lisa thought.

There were five children chasing each other around the stage. They were dressed in late nineteenth century clothes. Lisa watched them.

The fog machine began emitting large billows of mist into the audience. It was malfunctioning and making intermittent clanging noises. Visibility to the front of the stage got worse until the machine stopped with the sound of a fuse blowing. All the lights in the room flickered. Gasps could be heard as some of the audience were impressed by the coincidental special effects.

Stretching in her seat, Lisa counted five smaller black wispy shadows swaying in front of the stage. Each one of them stood out against the whiteness of the mist. More began to emerge but vanished as though realising that they had appeared in the wrong place. They weren't the only ones to disappear. Damian was gone. Lisa furrowed her brow. *Where did the priest go? And when?* She looked along the row. Nobody else seemed to have noticed. *Didn't he disturb anyone when he got up and left?*

A number of people sitting in front of the fog machine were coughing, but Pandora's attention was drawn to the small black shadows that were hovering several feet in front of her. She had never seen anything like them before.

Linda and Larry watched as the small black shadows changed into identical quintuplet figures. They looked like the five young men that Linda had seen going into Fred's shop on the day of his death. They remained still and appeared to be waiting for further instructions.

"I'm getting a number of messages coming through and they're eager to speak to some of you." Pandora's voice was no longer confident. She sounded panicked. Coughing, she cleared her throat and continued, "They're all trying to come through at the same time." Her smile was gone, and it looked like she might run. "You need to slow down. Can't you just talk to me, one at a time? I can't understand what it is that you're all trying to say." She began waving her arms in the air as though trying to push the voices away.

One of the quintuplets drifted away from the other four and hovered in front of Martyn. Later, it was to take his soul. Didn't he want to die anyway?

Mel jumped up. "Is one of them my Vicky?" She swayed from side to side as she waited for Pandora to respond.

Pandora had not heard Mel's voice over the commotion of the spirits.

Ben and Amanda had not noticed that Mel was there. They had not seen her arrive. Both of them looked around, at the same time when they heard her voice before they attempted to shrink into their seats.

"Please tell her that I still love her, I miss her dearly and think about her every day." Mel's facial expression turned to one of disappointment. She glanced sideways at Lisa, slumped her shoulders and sat down on her seat.

For a moment, Pandora looked like she might lose control. She took a deep breath, put her hands over her ears and closed her eyes. Whispers could be heard coming from the audience. The majority of them had not witnessed either the orbs, black shadow, children playing or the young men standing at the front. They were left feeling confused and wondered what was happening.

The second quintuplet drifted away from the remaining three and hovered in front of Mrs Blake. It was to take her soul. She was going to pass away in her sleep that night anyway.

Pandora's eyes opened and looked like they might pop out of her face. She was trying to ignore the supernatural entities that were present and focused her attention on the faces of the audience that were sitting on the second row. She feigned a smile. "Do we have someone with the initial 'R' in the room?" Her audience quietened, but it was difficult to gauge if anyone did or if they did not want to respond, out of fear. "A man... widower? I have a Dana... no wait... a Diane wanting to speak to him." Her arms were outstretched, and she wriggled her fingers as though she were picking the names from out of the air.

Is that Robert's late wife that's trying to get in touch with him? Lisa looked around the room. *Hang on a minute. That's how these so-called psychics reel you in. They throw random letters and names into the audience and wait for someone to take the bait.* She smiled and nodded. *That's clever, but I'm not going to fall for it.*

The rest of the audience were shaking their heads.

"Okay, maybe that person isn't here with us today," Pandora said. "My apologies, I don't always get it right."

The pleasant aromas of the evening meal were beginning to fade. They were being replaced by the usual smells that are produced when there is a room full of adults with no open doors or windows.

The remaining three quintuplets drifted away from the front of the stage and hovered in front of Ben and Amanda. They were to take their souls as they were supposed to die on the day of that picnic, near the waterfall.

Closing her eyes, Pandora placed the palm of her hand onto her forehead as though it somehow enhanced her psychic ability.

Lisa looked around the room. *I wish I'd got myself another drink now. I wonder what this lot think of this Paranormal Pandora and what's happening? Or not, as the case would seem. I wonder if they're thinking the same as me. I can see that there are spirits in the room, but can anyone else see them?*

Mel sat upright as she continued to stare at Pandora. She was hoping to receive a message from either Vicky or George.

Pandora moved her hand away from her forehead. Her eyes remained closed as she spoke, "Is there someone in this room who goes by the name of Lisa?" Her voice had deepened and for the first time that evening, she had Lisa's undivided attention.

Lisa did not answer, but she was sure that the rest of the room had heard her gulp. *It's a popular name. There could easily be more than one of us sitting in this room. Brenda on reception as probably got a list of people that are attending. She's just passed it onto Pandora.*

"Lisa, I know that you're in here. I can see you." Pandora's eyes remained closed as she spoke.

The audience began to look around the room. Lisa remained still as though any sudden movement would give away her position. Derek turned around and caught sight of her. He recognised her as the young lady that had knocked on his front door and introduced herself. He turned back to look at Pandora and said nothing to the others.

Lisa continued to listen, but she needed a definite sign.

"I need you to listen to me, Lisa."

Is this message definitely aimed at me? It must be. Am I supposed to be able to tell who that voice belongs to? It became apparent to Lisa that the others in the room were oblivious to Pandora's words as they began moving in slow motion at a speed that would suggest that time was almost standing still for them. She saw Damian standing next to the fire exit and he was staring at her.

Lisa put up her hand, like she was back in the classroom, and said, "I'm Lisa, but apparently you already know that, and you are?"

"There are a few of us here, Lisa. We need you to listen and hopefully cooperate with us. We can't force you, but you are the only one that can put a stop to it." Pandora's ample bosom rose as she took a deep breath.

Lisa shrugged. "You still haven't answered my question. Who are you?"

"If I told you who I was, you wouldn't listen to what I have to say."

"I won't listen if you don't!"

Pandora pointed towards the back corner of the room. "Those are your grandparents, Lisa. They want you to help free your father, Peter."

Free him? Lisa turned to look at Fred and Katherine. They were almost transparent, but she could make out their faces. She recognised Fred. Smiling, she nodded at both of them.

"I believe that you already know Vicky." Pandora pointed at her. She had appeared and was standing to the side of Damian.

Lisa looked over at Vicky. *Poor girl, she looks so unhappy.* Vicky was beginning to fade.

Pandora continued, "Vicky's mother, Mel, is sitting right next to you."

Lisa felt like she was being cornered and there was no means of escape. *Damn, I knew I should have left while I still had the chance.* She turned to look at Mel, but she was distant and unaware of what was going on as she continued to stare at Pandora. Turning around to check behind her, Lisa noticed that the black shadow was gone. It had left her to fend for herself.

"And in answer to your question, I'm John, the man that raised you," Pandora stated.

Lisa did not recognise the voice. It did sound similar to John's, but the tone was gentler and calmer. She could only remember his angry side. *Why are there so many spirits in this one room? Are they all here just for me? Why doesn't Vicky try to speak to her mother and tell her that I saw everything and did nothing to help her? And why isn't Fred angry with John?*

Pandora's legs tingled as she lowered herself onto the stage. With her knees bent, she pulled off her shoes, crossed her ankles to the side and began rubbing her feet. She continued, "Lisa, whatever has happened in the past needs to be left there. I need you to put it all to the back of your mind."

How can he dismiss everything that he's done so easily? Anyway, what the hell would he have to say to me that would be of any interest? Perhaps at some point he might actually decide to make an apology. Lisa did not want to cause a scene. She waited for him to continue.

"I know what you think of me, but you have to listen."

Lisa was growing restless. She folded her arms. "Go on."

Pandora was weakening. John knew that he did not have long. The lights in the room flickered. "That sycamore tree in Beechwood Park must be destroyed."

"Which sycamore tree? Why?"

"You know which one, Lisa. The one that has a pentangle on its trunk." Pandora's head flopped to one side as though it had become heavy. "Chop it down and destroy it, along with the roots."

Lisa's brow furrowed. "But, why? Do you know how ridiculous you sound? Why do *I* have to be the one to do it? I'm not a lumberjack!"

"Because, Peter is trapped until you do."

"And why would you care about what happens to Peter? He wouldn't have become trapped in the first place if you hadn't murdered him."

"Because that's his portal and it's seriously damaged." Pandora's head fell forward again. The lights in the room went out.

"You're unhinged. Have you heard yourself? What sort of game are you playing?" Lisa rose from her seat and made her way to the front of the stage.

"Just do what I ask, Lisa, before it's too late."

Pandora felt lightheaded as the walls and ceiling appeared to draw closer. Exhausted, she crumpled.

The wine bottle toppled. Its contents spilled over the table and trickled over the edge. The bottle did not roll; however, the wine glass crashed onto the table and smashed into tiny fragments. The bottle rose several feet into the air. It spun and flew with speed over the heads of the audience and towards the back wall where it shattered on impact.

The door at the side of the stage began to open. The spirits disappeared. Brenda popped her head around the door. Her timing was perfect as Pandora and her audience appeared to come back to life. Most of them seemed unaware of what had happened.

Pandora lifted her head and looked at Lisa. She was surprised to see her out of her seat and standing in front of the stage. She got to her feet, looked around for her shoes and picked them up.

"Sorry to disturb you, Pandora, but I've got a very distressed lady on the telephone who is desperately wanting to speak to a Lisa Brook." Brenda's look suggested that she felt awkward.

Pandora looked at Brenda with a vacant expression.

Lisa put up her hand. "That's me." She collected her belongings from her seat and followed Brenda to the reception.

Brenda reached over the reception desk and passed Lisa the telephone handset.

"Hi, Mum." Lisa glanced across at Brenda who had started to shuffle some paperwork about on her desk.

"Lisa... how did you know that it was me?" Elizabeth sniffled. "I never told the lady that picked up the phone who I was."

"Lucky guess. Why didn't you ring me on my mobile?"

"I've tried, but I couldn't get through to you. It kept going through to your voicemail and you know how I feel about leaving messages on them things."

Lisa looked at Brenda who was now filing her already pristine nails. "Listen, Mum. Is it okay if I ring you back in a minute? I'll go up to my room and call you from my mobile."

"Okay, but please don't be long."

Lisa handed the handset to Brenda. "Thank you."

Funny that I never heard my phone ring. Lisa walked towards the lift and pulled her mobile from her handbag. It was laying on top of her purse. She looked at its screen. *Strange! The battery's not flat and there are no missed calls.* The lift was out of action, so she had to take the stairs.

Throwing her bag onto the bed, Lisa rang Elizabeth.

"Lisa, is that you? You took your time."

"Sorry about that, Mum. The lift's not working. Is everything all right? Are you and Peter okay?"

"Yes... Peter and I are both fine, but...," Elizabeth paused and sniffled before she continued, "there's been a terrible accident." The line went quiet.

Lisa could hear that Elizabeth had started to wheeze. *Hope she doesn't go and have one of her asthma attacks on me.* She remained quiet and waited, but it felt like an age. *Something must have happened to Robert.*

"Oh Lisa... Susan's body was found in the lake." Elizabeth began to cry. "Did you hear me? I said your sister's dead."

"Dead?" *What the fuck!*

"You don't seem very shocked," Elizabeth sniffled.

"Of course I am." *Bloody hell, Mum. Give me a little bit of time to process what you've just said.* "I don't know what to say. I'm really sorry, but I've been drinking. I'm over the limit, so I won't be able to drive up there tonight to collect Peter."

"Oh, don't worry about Peter. He can keep me company and stay with me for as long as you want. Just come up when you're ready."

"Did Peter see Susan's body?" *Please tell me that he didn't.*

"I'm not sure." Elizabeth gulped out loud. "Peter was having a drink of juice in the kitchen when Susan's body was recovered."

"Did she drown?" *But I'm sure that Susan was a good swimmer.*

"They're not sure. She's got some other horrific injuries too. She was sitting by the lake, reading Peter a story. I went up into the house to get him another book. I'd only been gone a couple of minutes. When I asked him where Susan was, he said that he didn't know."

So, Peter was probably left on his own and next to the water. It could so easily have been him that drowned. "Okay, Mum, please keep a close eye on him. I'll be there as soon as I can. I've got something that I need to sort out first."

Chapter Fifteen
Farewell 'Susan'

Elizabeth had been sitting on her usual seat at the bottom of the garden with a throw draped over her legs. She would look up from her book occasionally to glance over at Susan and Peter. Susan was sitting with her legs dangling over the side of the jetty. Her toes were dipped in the water as she read to Peter. He was sitting, cross-legged, by her side and leaning with his elbow resting on her thigh. Looking at the pictures in the book, he would giggle when she changed her voice for the different characters.

The wine was going down freely. Elizabeth folded the corner of her page, closed the book and placed it on top of the table to the side of her empty wine glass and bottle. As she looked up, she noticed that a boat was passing, close by. It stopped and the man that was on board appeared to be waving at Susan. She stopped reading to Peter, mid-sentence, to signal the man back. Elizabeth did not recognise him.

"Grandma, please can I have another book?" Peter asked. "This one's getting boring." He emphasised the word 'boring' before he placed a hand over his mouth and pretended to yawn.

Getting up, Elizabeth placed the throw over the back of her seat. "Yes, sweetheart, but this will have to be the last one because it's nearly your bedtime." *I'll nip down into the cellar and get another bottle of wine for Susan and me. I need to try and find out why her marriage has really broken down.*

Peter watched as the man in the boat blew his Auntie Susan a kiss. He screwed up his face and watched as she puckered her lips and blew him one back. "Yuck!" The boat drifted closer. *That's not Uncle Karl.* He knew who he was. *It's that man from the café. I don't like him.*

Peter stood and walked away from Susan. He went to sit on his grandmother's seat. "Go away," he yelled at the man.

Susan turned to Peter. "Excuse me, young man. Don't be so rude."

Closing his eyes, Peter shouted, "No... I don't like that man. Make him go away, Auntie Susan."

Jumping up, Susan paced across to Peter. She leant forward and put her face close to his. "Apologise now, Peter!" she ordered.

Peter could feel the warmth of Susan's alcohol tainted breath on his face. When he opened his eyes, they were met with her stare. Wiping away her spittle with the palm of his hand, he said, "No."

Susan reached out and gripped the tops of Peter's arms. She yanked him from the seat and his little body was pulled through the air as though he were a rag doll.

She did it with such force that it caused his collar to rub against the back of his neck and it left behind a friction burn.

"Go into the house immediately, Peter," a deep voice bellowed. It sounded to be coming from the top of the garden. "Get away from that water."

Susan was holding Peter in the air with his legs dangling beneath him. He did not put up a fight, but instead pressed his lips together. When she heard the voice, she let him go and as he fell onto the jetty, he bumped his knees. He wanted to cry but stopped himself.

Turning around to look for who was calling him, Peter could not see anyone and did not recognise the voice. He got onto his feet, picked up his book, ran up the garden and into the house before whoever it was got the chance to shout at him again.

Susan stood there for a moment longer and waited for someone to appear. She could not see anyone, but she felt something press against her chest as it pushed against her. Her hands came up to push it away, but there was nothing there as she waved her arms about in front of her. Her feet slid until her heels were overhanging the edge of the jetty. The pressure on her chest stopped and she tried to balance herself with her toes trying to grip hold of the wooden planks, but with that one final shove she plunged into the water.

Bill had heard that voice and watched as Peter scarpered. He saw Susan fall, but did not try to help her.

He made the fateful decision to turn on the boat's engine and steer away.

The sky had darkened, and thunder could be heard rumbling in the distance. The storm looked to be fast heading Susan's way.

Susan's face emerged above the surface of the water. She had only been under for several seconds but came up gasping for air. She moved her eyes from side to side as she looked for Bill. *Where is he? I can't see him. He's left me on my own.* "Help!" A gentle ripple washed over her face and into her open mouth. The water tasted foul as it slithered down her throat. She began to cough. *I need to stop. I'm disturbing the water. Why are my eyes sore and why does everything look so blurry?* "Can anyone hear me?" *Maybe someone's already on their way.* She needed to get to the jetty and climb up, but she could not move. Standing on her tiptoes, she could feel herself sinking into the sludge at the bottom of the lake. *What's that smell? It seems to be getting stronger. I've smelt it somewhere before.*

Susan recognised it. It was the same smell that greeted you when you filled your car at the petrol station.

Bill's boat was oozing fuel.

Keeping her head still, Susan looked sideways. A tall dark silhouette stood to the far end of the jetty. *Someone's here to help me.* She could not make out their face. "Thank, God," she said, "I'm freezing, and I'm stuck."

The figure did not move as though it was unsure what to do.

"Mum… is that you?" *I can't hear anything!* Susan's ears were beneath the water. "Can you get the lifebuoy from Robert's boat and throw it to me?" she asked. "I know that you're afraid of the water, but you don't need to get in. I'm sure I can manage to get myself out." The figure moved towards the boat. *Shit, that's not Mum. She'd be panicking and screaming by now. Who the hell is it?* "Help!" But her cries were stifled as water lapped over her face.

The lifebuoy landed at Susan's side; it was within her reach, but she could not get to it. *My arms won't move. I'm paralysed.* Her heart was racing, and her stomach felt heavy as she tried to keep her face above the water, but it was no use, she was sinking. *I'm drowning. I don't want to die!* "Please, God, I'm sorry for all the bad things that I've done."

It was moments later when the black shadow chose to make its move. It lowered itself from the boat, stopped short of her and hovered before it released her from the sludge. She was not able to move as she floated on her back and looked up, through smarting eyes, in horror, at what had freed her. *Fuck me, it's not even human. What the hell is that thing?* She wanted to scream but couldn't. *Why can't I move or speak any more? I need to get out of here. I just know that it's going to kill me.*

The air and surrounding water were toxic. Susan watched as the black shadow threw a match into the air. It ignited. Thunder rumbled overhead as fork lightning cracked open the sky. A look of sheer panic washed over her face when she realised that these were to be her final moments. The fire roared towards her as the surrounding water bubbled beneath the flames. She gasped for breath, but it was useless as the fire took hold of her body.

Elizabeth gave the cellar door another push, but this time she had charged at it with her shoulder. It opened. She fell through the doorway, picked herself up and walked up the steps and into the kitchen. The rain was lashing against the windows. Peter was sitting, cross-legged, in the open doorway and watching as the lightning struck the lake. She looked around the kitchen. "Peter, where's your Auntie Susan?"

Peter did not answer. He was not listening. He was mesmerised by nature's spectacular display of power.

Elizabeth crouched next to Peter. She put her hand on his shoulder and asked him again where his Auntie Susan was.

Without speaking, Peter pointed towards the lake.

"She's not still out in this weather, is she?" Elizabeth asked. She put the bottle of wine on the kitchen work surface and shouted out of the door, "Susan, come inside or you'll catch your death."

It was hard for Elizabeth to determine if Susan had heard her through the rumblings of thunder, but there did not appear to be any response.

The storm was passing as Elizabeth walked down to the jetty. "Bloody hell, Susan. What are you playing at? I hope you're not still flirting with that man on that boat," she grumbled to herself.

When Elizabeth reached the water there was no sign of Susan. The fire had died down, but visibility, because of the smoke, remained poor. There was the smell of burnt meat drifting through the air. *Smells like someone's having a barbeque.* She climbed onto Robert's boat and tried to look out over the water. *Maybe she's gone off with that man in the boat. Strange, I thought she might have had the decency to mention it though. Maybe she tried but couldn't find me because I was stuck in the cellar or maybe Peter is just being a little monkey and she's already inside the house.*

Peter had followed Elizabeth to the lake. He was waiting for his grandmother to witness what was floating in the water in front of him. He never made a sound as he continued to point at what was left of his Auntie Susan. Her charred corpse was smouldering.

Peering over the side of the boat, Elizabeth yelled when she saw Peter, "Get away from the water. Go back into the house where you'll be safe." She gestured frantically for him to move away.

But Peter did not move. He continued to point and stare with a look of determination. Elizabeth followed his line of sight and when she caught sight of the corpse, she screamed.

Within seconds, Elizabeth was standing at Peter's side. She was terrified that he might fall into the water. She picked him up and noticed the burn on the back of his neck. She turned his head away, blocking his view of the body and held him tight.

On the other side of the lake there appeared to be a boat in flames.

Elizabeth stared into the water. Her mind was confused, and her heart was tearing in two, but she needed to keep it together for Peter's sake. "Did you try and save your Auntie Susan? Is that why you have a burn on your neck?"

Peter looked puzzled. *I didn't help. I'm too small. It was Auntie Susan that hurt my neck.* "No."

"Did you throw the lifebuoy from Robert's boat into the water?"

Looking towards the water, Peter wanted to know what a lifebuoy looked like. "No." He shook his head.

Elizabeth turned Peter's head to divert his eyes. "But if you didn't throw it in, then who did?"

"I don't know," Peter shrugged. He began to shiver.

The black shadow was next to Robert's boat. It remained still as though it was gauging Elizabeth's reaction. She looked at it, but her attention was drawn away by what sounded like Susan gasping for air. *That noise can't have come from her. It's not possible. No, I imagined it.* Was it wrong for her to feel relief that it

241

was not Susan fighting for her life? What type of existence would she have endured if she had survived such a horrific accident?

There was no sign of the black shadow when Elizabeth turned back around to look. *Maybe it's gone on board the boat. I don't really care.* She ran back up the garden with Peter in her arms, ran into the house, locked the door behind her and rang for an ambulance.

Chapter Sixteen
Enlightenment

Lisa lay on her bed and stared up at the ceiling. Her head spun and it was not from the side effects of the alcohol. She had not had a lot to drink. It was on account of Susan being dead and that strange conversation she'd had earlier with Pandora. *Did Susan drown? I wonder what those other injuries were that Mum was talking about. What's happened exactly? And how am I supposed to chop down that sycamore tree? It's in a public park. How am I meant to explain that one to the council?* As far as Lisa was aware you could not just go around and cut down random trees on the say-so of a psychic. Not even a tree that is a gateway to another dimension. *None of it makes any sense.*

Larry had heard the whole conversation between Lisa and Pandora. He had noticed that everyone around him had acted out in slow motion throughout the deliverance of the message. He had remained still, so as not to draw attention to himself.

"I would like to thank you all for coming this evening," Pandora announced. "But, unfortunately, I'm going to have to call it a night. I'm feeling a little under the weather."

Pandora's audience began to leave. Some of them sounded despondent with words of protest whilst others looked at her with puzzled expressions. They believed her to be intoxicated. Most of them would descend on an unsuspecting Brenda at the reception desk and demand full refunds.

Larry remained seated. He leant across Sylvia so that he could speak to Derek. He was concerned that he may be overheard. "I've got a job for you," he whispered.

Thinking it an unusual time and place to discuss his work, Derek replied, "Oh?" He furrowed his brow as he looked at Larry.

"It's something that needs to be done quickly." There was an urgency to Larry's tone as he spoke louder.

"What does?" Derek still looked puzzled.

"A sycamore tree that's in Beechwood Park needs to be chopped down and its roots must be destroyed."

"A tree that's actually in the grounds of a public park and that's looked after by the local council? And does the tree in question have a T.P.O?"

Larry screwed up his face. "A what?"

"A Tree Preservation Order."

"I've no idea." Larry shrugged. *I don't even know what one of them is and I don't really care.*

"Why would you want to destroy a perfectly healthy tree?"

"I'll help you." Larry was trying to divert the conversation away from Derek's questioning.

"We'll need to make the necessary checks first. I don't fancy being landed with a hefty fine and a criminal record."

Sylvia intervened. She had not heard the conversation between Lisa and Pandora but assumed that a similar discussion to the one at the séance must have taken place. "Perhaps we should do it tonight while the park is empty," she suggested.

"What's the hurry?" Derek found the whole conversation ridiculous and laughed. "We can't do it tonight. It's not possible. It could take us a while to get the necessary authority."

"I don't think you'd believe us if we told you," Sylvia replied.

Derek folded his arms. "Try me."

"I should probably have told you earlier about what went on at that séance in our house... but, to cut a long story short... our house is haunted." Sylvia was matter-of-fact.

Is that why Sylvia acted like she did when Lisa came to our door? Her name must have cropped up. "Oh, I already know that," Derek said. "We talked about it briefly the other night but didn't discuss it in any great detail. Don't you remember? I think you were surprised that I agreed with you, but I still don't understand what that has to do with chopping down a sycamore tree in the local park."

245

"What exactly have you seen?" Sylvia asked.

"I've seen a black shadow on two separate occasions. I don't know if it's the same one, though."

"When?"

"The same day that you did. When I went to lock the back door, I saw it making its way into the garden and it was in the corner of our kitchen. It watched me as I tidied away the plates later on that same evening."

Larry interrupted, "That's how the spirit that haunts your house travels between dimensions. Its portal is the sycamore tree with the pentangle carved into it. Another spirit that's in your home warned us. A spirit that passed away in your home."

Derek thought for a moment. *It's clear that, with or without me, they're determined that the tree's got to go and they're just going to continue to ignore what I have to say. I've got no choice; I'm going to have to help them. After all, what do they know about cutting down a tree?* "Sound travels further at night, so we won't be able to use any power tools, or we'll be heard by the nearby houses," he conceded. "It'll need to be an axe. It'll take us longer, but we could take it in turns; however, it'll probably take us all night."

Most of Pandora's other guests had now left the room.

Martyn remained motionless in his wheelchair.

Mr & Mrs Cooper's lifeless bodies were still holding hands.

The young man who had been sitting next to Mrs Blake was trying to waken her, by shaking her shoulder.

Mel had left, disappointed.

Visibility and lighting were limited at the park. The sounds of the local wildlife had fallen silent. Sylvia, Larry, June and Linda were hiding behind a huge rhododendron bush. Why? Not one of them had bothered to question. They were waiting for Derek who had dashed home to collect an axe and a torch.

What's keeping my Derek? He's been gone for ages. I hope that he hasn't changed his mind. No, I'm sure that he wouldn't let me down.

The ground began to shake as a thickening mist started to appear around their feet. Minor tremors were rare in Beechwood, but several had been known to take place over the years.

Linda was the first one to notice that something was writhing about their ankles. It was twisting and brushing against them like gentle waves. Without looking, she realised what was there and screamed. She began to perspire, and her breathing became erratic. *I'm sure those damn snakes can sense my fear, but I can't help it.* She cupped her hands over her ears as their hissing got louder.

Sylvia looked at Linda, wide eyed. She could hear the snakes, but not to the same deafening pitch. She had her own concerns as someone or something was touching her arm, but the movement felt wrong for it to be a snake. It was comparable to fingertips tapping, one by one, whilst they moved up her arm. She looked as she wanted to know how many snakes there were, what type, how big they were and if any of them were venomous. But it would have been impossible to tell as the snakes were not visible through the mist which had risen halfway up their shins. It was her turn to yell as her eyes fell on a spider that was crawling up her arm and making its way towards her face. It was huge, hairy and hideous. It reared up onto its back legs as it got ready to attack. Opening its disproportionate mouth to reveal blood stained fangs, it launched itself at her neck and pierced her with two holes. She shrieked and knocked it off with the back of her hand.

June was scratching her head. Her scalp was itching, and she tried, in vain, to relieve it. Her head was covered with thousands of insects that were crawling and clambering over each other. She stopped scratching and her hair continued to move by itself. As she leant forward and brushed her fingers through her hair some of the creatures fell to the ground and became lost to the mist while others clung to the roots, bit into her scalp and started on their journey, burrowing deep. She felt every movement. Panicking, she dug her fingernails into her scalp and tried to gouge them out, but there were too many. They continued to tunnel inside her head. Her fingernails and hands were covered with crushed insects and pieces of her scalp as blood seeped down over her face.

Larry watched on in horror. He could not believe what he was seeing and did not know what to do. Closing his eyes, he counted to ten out loud and hoped that when he opened them everything would be back to how it was before. When he got to ten and opened his eyes, he noticed that nothing had changed.

The calming sounds of the river flowing behind June gave her a moment of inspiration. She needed to get into that water and make her way towards the waterfall. The flowing water was the only way that she would get rid of those creepy crawlies. It was a matter of feet away and she could be there within seconds. Turning around, she got ready to run, but her feet got tangled and she fell to the ground. The mist blanketed her.

Larry lunged. He needed to rescue June and without thinking, he put his hands down into the mist where she had fallen. He fumbled about until he found what he believed to be her arm and tried to pull her up. Sylvia and Linda did not dare to move. Larry had his hands around one of the snakes. Its head was huge with gigantic eyes and a wide mouth filled with serrated teeth, but it did not look like it belonged to the dark scaly body that was attached. He let it go and stood upright.

A faint circular light emerged at the far end of the footpath. It was Derek. He was holding a torch out in front of him. Step-by-step, its light became bigger and brighter. An axe dangled from his other hand, by his side. It was by no means the biggest of his collection, but it would do the job.

Derek was not alone, though. There was someone walking several feet behind him and the mist was clearing beneath that person's footsteps. Although, they were light on their feet, he sensed their presence and turned to see who it was. He shone the torch in her face and recognised the young lady that used to live in his house.

Dazzled by the light of the torch, Lisa put out her hand to block its glare. "Hi," she said, "sorry, I hope I didn't startle you."

Derek pointed his torch at the ground. "No, you didn't," he responded. "Although, I wasn't expecting to see you or anyone else down here at this time of night."

"Nor I." Lisa looked at the axe in his hand. She pointed to it and said, "What are you going to do with that? You're not here to cut down a sycamore tree, are you?"

"Yes, I am." Derek looked confused. "How did you know?"

"I think we might be here for the same reason, but I was under the impression that it was *my* responsibility to cut it down."

"I wouldn't know anything about that. You see, I'm not here by myself. There are some others that are waiting for me." Derek pointed along the footpath. "My wife and some of her friends."

Lisa looked at where Derek was pointing. She could see their silhouettes and nodded in response.

Derek noted that Lisa was not carrying any equipment. *How's she going to chop down a tree without any tools?*

"Are you going to allow me to pass?" Lisa raised her eyebrows and feigned a smile.

Derek quickly moved aside, as he had not intended to block her way on purpose. "Oh, I'm sorry." He gestured for Lisa to pass. He watched as she walked by and as she stepped into the mist, it moved aside ahead of her feet and began to clear. He followed her and started to believe that she was the one that could hold all the answers as to what was going on.

Glancing over her shoulder, Lisa answered Derek's query, though the question had never passed his lips and he had only thought it. "I hadn't realised that others knew about the sycamore tree. I never really intended to do the job myself. I'm just here to see what all the excitement is about."

"I'm only here under duress. Orders from the wife and her gang."

Lisa sniggered. "You live in my family's old house, don't you? You're that fella that answered the door when I knocked the other day."

"Ah, yes," Derek answered. "We had, well when I say we, I mean…"

Lisa stopped walking and turned around. "Go on," she said. "It's okay, I don't bite."

Derek smiled. He had started to sweat. "Sylvia had just held a séance and I believe that your name came up." He was aware that he had broken his wife's confidence.

"A séance in your home? So, when I turned up at your door, why didn't your wife want to know? Why did she turn me away? I only wanted to look at what you'd done to the place."

"Shock... I guess." Derek shrugged. "I don't know. Your timing was pretty unbelievable. Maybe it was all a little bit too much for her to take in."

"Do you know why my name popped up? Was there someone from the other side trying to get in touch with me?"

Derek did not answer. His expression was vacant.

Leave him alone, Lisa. He doesn't have a clue what's going on. It's his wife that's dragged him into this. She looked up at the full moon. It was helping to light her path. The mist along the ground had thinned and was clear of any snakes or arachnids.

Five black wispy shadows changed into quintuplets and hovered to the end of the path, near to the sycamore, as though they were on guard duty. The young men did not make eye contact with Lisa. They stared at the tree. She walked in front of them and looked at each of them in turn, like a corporal inspecting her platoon. Derek followed her.

Lisa approached the tree and looked at June who was lying face down over its protruding roots. Her body had been pulled there by the snakes that had writhed beneath the mist. The extent of her injuries were visible as the top of her head continued to be a frenzied feast. The insects had eaten through her skull and were starting to devour her brain as the sounds of chewing and grinding became frantic. Lisa did not seem concerned as Larry and Linda raced across and stood by June's side. They were scared and weren't sure what to do. What *could* they do?

Emerging from behind the rhododendron bush, Sylvia was not able to move any further. She opened her mouth and called out to Derek, but the sound of her voice faded away.

A number of spectators had arrived. Katherine was swaying on a swing with Fred pushing her from behind. Lisa caught sight of Damian who was perched on top of the climbing frame alongside Vicky. They watched Lisa with interest, as though they were waiting for something to happen.

Susan, who was by no means transparent, appeared at Lisa's side and the severity of her injuries were obvious for anyone that was able to see.

Lisa turned to look at her and she could not believe her eyes. "Jesus, look at the state of you. What the hell happened?"

Who's Lisa talking to? Derek thought.

Susan tried to embrace Lisa, but her arms passed through her. Lisa found the stench of her burnt flesh and her visible internal body parts overwhelming and could not stop herself from coughing. Susan backed away when she noted Lisa's repulsion.

Derek saw that Sylvia was standing alone, over by the bush, and ran across to be by her side. The palm of her hand was pressing against the side of her neck. "I'm sorry that I took so long," he began to explain. He looked at her with an expression of apprehension. "I couldn't find the right sized batteries for the torch. I thought there might have been some in my toolbox under the stairs, but they weren't there and as I was leaving, I found a new packet on the kitchen table. I thought it was a bit strange that they'd be there, though, as I swear, they weren't when I went in."

"Well, you're here now and that's all that matters." Sylvia tried to smile.

Gazing over at the havoc that was unfolding beneath the tree, Derek joked, "Have I missed much?" He was trying to keep Sylvia calm, but, in reality, he had just about shat himself when he saw what was happening to June.

"Yes, you could say that." A gooey mess of bloody pus began seeping out from between Sylvia's fingers and oozed over her forearm. "We must hurry and chop down that damn tree," she stated before gasping for breath.

"That can wait. What the hell have you done to yourself?" Derek put his hand up to move Sylvia's hand away from her neck. "Let me have a look."

At first, Sylvia was reluctant. She was scared of what would be revealed, but Derek kept his hand over the top of hers until she moved her hand away to show him the two infected fang lacerations. "It was a spider." The whites of her eyes were reddening, and her face glowed, with beads of perspiration appearing on her forehead. "You always told me that my phobia was irrational because they don't bite, well... surprise." She was not able to laugh. Her head and shoulders drooped forward. She felt suddenly very weak as her legs crumpled beneath her.

Derek managed to catch Sylvia before she hit the ground and eased her fall. He made sure that she was comfortable before he pulled a handkerchief from his trouser pocket. Opening the handkerchief, he folded it in half and placed it over her injury. "Can you hold it against the wound for me? We need to get you to a hospital." He tried to give her a reassuring smile. "And fast."

June's eyes opened at the same time as her body began to convulse. Foam oozed from her mouth. She began to choke. Larry was powerless to help. He wanted her to die, and quick, so that her torment would end. After all, how could anyone survive without the top of their head?

Shining his torch towards the tree, Derek shouted, "Has anybody rung for an ambulance, yet?" *Surely someone must have done. There's probably one already on the way for June.*

Larry did not hear Derek as he watched June take her last breath.

Reaching inside her jacket pocket, Linda pulled out a squashed packet of cigarettes. There were a couple left alongside a disposable lighter. She lit one of the cigarettes, inhaled and looked at her mobile telephone. Its battery was flat. Smoke escaped from her nostrils as she exhaled. "No," she called back in Derek's direction.

The tree illuminated red with an inferno of flames within. Linda and Larry stepped back as June began to disintegrate. Her body made a series of crackling noises, like a piece of meat cooking under a grill that is too hot. It would appear that the tree was not only taking souls, but it was now taking whatever was left of the bodies as well. It stopped glowing and returned to normal, now resembling any of the others next to it. There was no sign of June having ever been there.

"Can someone help me, *please*?" Derek yelled desperately. He was not aware of June's demise. His mobile telephone would not turn on and he needed to get Sylvia out of the park. The puncture marks on her neck were getting worse. The artery above where she held her hand was pulsating quicker and its deepening shade stood out against her pale skin. He did not want to leave her alone, but he needed to get to a payphone.

There was nothing that Linda could do to comfort Larry. He had closed himself off to the outside world as he stared aghast at where June had, only moments earlier, laid beneath the tree.

With the lit cigarette drooping from the corner of her mouth, Linda walked over to Derek. "June's gone." As she spoke, her cigarette bobbed up and down. Smoke puffed out of her mouth and nostrils. She started to cough.

Derek needed Linda to confirm what she had said. "Gone?" he questioned. He fanned her cigarette smoke away with the back of his hand and feigned a cough.

Looking at Sylvia, Linda said, "We watched as June died and then that tree took her for its own." Ash fell from the end of her cigarette and missed Sylvia's face by a couple of inches.

Derek was not convinced. *What's Linda going on about? How can a tree just take someone? What is it that she's smoking, exactly?*

Sylvia began to weep. The pain had become unbearable. She tried to stand, but her legs were numb. She started to slap her neck and each blow was harder than the one before, until they had turned into punches.

Grabbing Sylvia's wrist, Derek tried to stop her. "Stop it, you're hurting yourself," he shouted. "You're going to make it worse."

Shocked, Sylvia looked at Derek. He had never raised a hand to her in all the years that they had been together. "You're squeezing my arm, let go of me!" she exclaimed. She tried to pull her arm away, but he let go. At that exact moment, her arm became lifeless. "Now I can't move either of my arms."

"I'll run and get help," Linda wheezed. She scurried along the footpath with the unfinished cigarette placed firmly between her index and middle fingers.

Derek felt helpless. All he could do was sit with Sylvia until Linda brought help. He glanced over at Larry who looked to be standing in the same position with his head bowed. *We're just two men that are powerless to help their loved ones.* He looked around the park. *That's odd! Where did Lisa go?*

A thickening mist began to cover the ground as the temperature around them plummeted. "Get away, Derek," Sylvia said. Her voice was hoarse. "Get off the ground. Climb a tree. You've got to save yourself."

Despite what he had seen with his own eyes and everything that was going on around him, Derek still refused to believe that anything bad had happened. It had never crossed his mind that all of them might not get out of the park alive. "Save myself from what?" he asked. He rubbed his hands together in an attempt to warm them up. The vapour from his breath joined Sylvia's and the rising mist.

"Derek, just do what I ask," Sylvia pleaded, "there's not much time. The creatures that are under the mist are deadly."

"No, I'm not going to leave you." Derek held Sylvia's limp hand. He gave it a gentle squeeze. "I'm not afraid of any deadly creatures. Do you hear me? Now, say no more. That's the end of it."

Sylvia's puncture wounds had got bigger. She was melting. It was a delayed reaction to the spider's venom which was burning through and stopping at nothing. The poison continued into her bloodstream, which meant that she was dissolving on the inside. Perhaps it was a blessing that she was paralysed and unable to feel what lay ahead for her.

An acrid smell filled the air. Derek tried to clear his throat. He looked down at Sylvia, but she was no longer visible through the mist. The snakes had returned and were thrashing about, around them. He felt her hand being pulled away from his as her body was being moved towards the base of the tree. Reaching to grab her hand, he felt the movement of the creatures beneath the mist, but he did not care. He longed to follow her, but he was not able to move as his feet were being held to the ground. There was no reply when he shouted out her name, over and over again.

Larry was not aware that Sylvia was lying beneath the tree until it started to glow red. It was the exact spot where June had died. Sylvia was a few feet away from where he was standing when she passed away and her body faded, as though she had never existed.

The wind howled through the trees and rattled their branches as the moon's light became veiled behind an approaching sinister black cloud. The mist along the ground cleared and the creatures beneath were gone.

Derek was able to move again. He scrambled about on the ground until he found his axe and the torch.

Picking them up, he ran, like an escaped lunatic from an asylum, towards the tree. He struck its trunk with his axe. "Give me my wife back," he yelled. "I know you've got her."

Larry lunged and grabbed the torch from Derek's hand. He aimed its light at the trunk and watched as Derek hacked the tree. He was walloping it hard, one blow after another.

Moving like synchronised swimmers, the quintuplets repositioned. They hovered a few inches above the ground. They were several feet behind Larry, spread equally apart in an arc that surrounded one half of the tree. Their expressions remained impartial as they continued to stare ahead and watch as Derek tried to chop down the tree.

In a weakened state, Derek realised that all his effort was wasted. Each time he hit the axe against the trunk only a small chip was hacked away, which would regenerate straight away. It was like no other tree he had ever felled and had a hardened structure that was set like concrete.

Larry handed Derek the torch, took the axe from him and tried chopping, over and over again, but to no avail.

Clambering down from the climbing frame, Damian and Vicky strolled over to the swings and stood near to Fred and Katherine. Susan was close by. Each of them had an expression of concern, as though they were aware of what would happen next.

Lisa had returned and was standing behind the spectators. She had gone to sit by the river as she had needed time to think. She now knew what needed to be done. The truth was that she had always known.

Feeling Lisa's presence, all of the spirits turned to look at her.

Another spectator had arrived in the park. He was next to Susan. "Why's he here?" Lisa asked as she pointed at John.

"Don't be like that, Lisa. He's our father," Susan answered. "He's just here to make sure that you do the right thing and destroy that tree."

"Oh." Lisa feigned a shocked expression. "It's becoming quite an obsession with him. He'd really like me do that, wouldn't he? But, you've absolutely no idea why, have you, Susan?"

"Who is Lisa talking to?" Derek asked Larry as he squinted into the darkness. "Is it my Sylvia?"

"No, I think it's her sister," Larry answered. He was trying to listen to the conversation that was going on between Lisa and Susan.

"I can't see her," Derek interrupted. "Who's she talking about?"

"Not sure." Larry turned to look at Derek. "I think they're talking about their father. I presume that he's the man that's standing with them."

"I can't see him either. How do you know all this? I take it that you can hear them, as well as see them."

Larry did not answer.

Derek considered that all that was going on around him was just simply a nightmare. Closing his eyes, he tried to force himself to waken. He imagined that when he opened his eyes, he would be at home in their bed with Sylvia laying by his side.

Needless to say, it did not work. Derek opened his eyes and realised that it was not a bad dream. It was, in fact, a living hell. *What should I do? Should I run? But what will happen to Sylvia when she comes back and I'm not here?*

"Know about what?" Susan turned to look at John. Was he aware of what Lisa was insinuating? "All I know is that these people have tried to cut down the tree and failed. They will never succeed because it needs to be you," Susan pleaded. "And now three more people have died for nothing."

"Three! Who's the third?" Larry shouted.

Susan pointed at the branch of a nearby tree. Larry and Lisa turned and looked to see Linda's body hanging upside down. Her arms dangled beside where her head should have been. That was on the ground below and covered in dirt and foliage after rolling several feet.

Linda had managed to get as far as the gatepost at the entrance of the park when the creatures beneath the mist took her and hauled her along the gravel. One of the snakes had coiled itself around her head, so that her screams went unheard, before it bit it off and spat it out again.

Derek turned and examined the tree. He was intrigued. He wanted to know what Larry and Lisa were looking at. Stepping back, he tilted his head to one side as fear coursed through his body. *There isn't any help on the way. Why have I been so blind? It was so obvious and staring me right in the face. Why didn't I persuade Sylvia not to get involved? If our house really is haunted, then we could just have moved on. Now, I've lost her and I'm going to need to arrange her funeral. How can I though when there isn't even a body? Maybe that's because she isn't really dead!* He could not get the latter thought out of his mind.

Lisa moved closer to Susan and asked, "Why do you think that it needs to be me that cuts down that tree? Have you not even, just once, asked yourself that question? Are you not in the least bit intrigued?" She paused for a moment to give her chance to answer. "I can tell you that I was to start with. John hoped that I'd just do what he said with no further thought or questions asked."

Susan shook her head and shrugged.

"Why don't you ask Daddy," Lisa said, "he knows all too well. He might even give you a little hint if you ask him ever so nicely."

Susan turned to look at John. She looked like she might cry. "Dad, what's Lisa talking about? What do you know that I don't? Why is she acting like this?"

"In all honesty, it's been coming back to me, bit by bit, over the last few years," Lisa interrupted before

263

John got a chance to answer. She put the palm of her hand in front of his face. "I was controlled, you see, and made to feel absolutely worthless. I wasn't allowed to think for myself and beaten so that I wouldn't be able to remember." She paced before stopping in front of the tree. "And then, as if by magic, I've only gone and remembered everything."

"Remembered what exactly?" Susan asked.

"Oh, and by the way, before I forget to mention it. Why didn't you tell me that you were seeing Bill? And, please, don't make out that you hadn't realised who he was."

Susan's mouth gaped. Perhaps some sort of an explanation was about to be confessed, but not one single word managed to pass her lips.

Imitating Susan's facial expression, Lisa sniggered before saying, "Now, let me guess, I'd say that judging from the look on what's left of your face, you hadn't realised that I knew about your affair."

Susan looked at the ground and it was not out of shame. It was because someone had managed to catch her out on her devious behaviour.

"I saw you carrying on with Bill and it was only moments before Karl picked you up. Did you want him to catch you at it? I don't even want to know how long it was going on. I dread to think. I just want you to answer me one thing. Why did you choose him, Susan?"

Susan did want to answer, but the words would not come out. Her mouth opened and closed, and it made her look like a goldfish that was searching for food in its tank.

"Did you want him just because he used to be mine? Would you like me to reunite you both? I can easily arrange it." Lisa walked over to Linda's head, picked it up by her hair and drop kicked it over the trees, as though it were a football. It landed with a splash in the river.

"He was married to someone else. He never really was yours," Susan remarked as she watched Lisa walk towards her.

Lisa nodded in agreement because it was hard for her to deny that Susan's words were indeed very true. *But why's she talking about Bill in the past tense?* "Was?"

"You don't know, do you?" A smug expression started to appear on Susan's face, but she managed to stop herself from smiling.

"Know what?"

"Bill's dead."

Lisa shook her head. *No, that's not true. He can't be dead. Susan's just trying to wind me up.* "Really? How? When?"

"Bill's boat got damaged, somehow, and it was leaking fuel. It set on fire and the rest is history. He died on the lake at the same time as I did."

Lisa took a moment to take in what Susan had told her before she asked, "Where's Bill now?"

"He's waiting for me."

"Is he coming here, or can't he be bothered?"

"No, he doesn't need to. None of this concerns him."

The quintuplets turned to their left and drifted towards the swings. They stopped in front of the spectators to obstruct their view. This was a stark warning. It was time for them to move on.

"It's time that we were on our way, Fred," Katherine said. "There's nothing we can do to stop the inevitable from happening. I thought that if our granddaughter saw us, it might sway her to make the right decision, but it wasn't to be." They moved several feet before they vanished.

Vicky's attempt at escaping purgatory had failed. She ascended, hovering horizontally in mid-air and moved towards the river to become its prisoner again. Damian followed her to the edge of the water. He transformed into an entity, sprouted his wings and watched on helpless. She floated into the distance and re-emerged beneath the waterfall. This was a scene that would replay for an eternity unless that cursed tree was destroyed in its entirety and it would allow her soul to be released. He extended his wings and soared into the sky.

Turning to look at Larry, Lisa took his hand and shook it. She smiled and said, "Thank you."

Larry was confused.

Derek looked suspicious. *Why's Lisa thanking Larry? Hang on a minute, he's in on the whole thing.*

No wonder he was just standing around and looking like a spare part. Before Derek realised what he was doing and without giving it any further consideration, he picked up his axe and lunged it into the top of Larry's skull. His head opened up like a watermelon and his legs crumpled beneath him. He fell short of the tree's roots. Lisa shoved him with her foot so that the tree could get a better hold. The tree lit up and he was gone within seconds.

A black shadow appeared and towered over Lisa. It waited by her side for her instructions. Derek had not been able to see the spirits that were around him; however, he could not fail to notice this one. He stood back and began to take small steps as he needed to get a better look at what was in front of him. His mouth gaped in awe. *What the hell is that thing? I've seen something like it before at home. It might even be the same one.* There was nowhere for him to go. He fell with his back against the tree.

The black shadow leant forward until its head was close to Derek's face. Tilting its head from one side to the other, it considered what its next move might be. It could see the sweaty glow on his brow and smell the fear that was oozing from his pores. It drew back.

"I'm sorry that you were the one to move into my old home," Lisa said to Derek.

Derek was too scared to speak.

"And that your wife was rude to my son and me."

Twisting itself, the black shadow looked over in John and Susan's direction. It moved towards them, like a cat stalking a mouse, until it was in front of them.

The tree began to pulsate. A rhythmic beat sounded out. Its inner fire lit up the darkness. Derek tried to pull himself away from the soaring heat but struggled as the tree held him back. The harder he fought, the more he found himself being pulled into its trunk.

"I'm sorry that it's come to this," Lisa said, although her expression would suggest to the contrary. "All I ever wanted to do was sit down and talk to you and your wife about buying back my family's old home, but you wouldn't even allow me to have a look around."

"Lisa, stop!" Susan shouted. "What the hell are you doing?"

Lisa turned to look at Susan. She began to laugh. The black shadow returned and waited by her side. "My dear, Susan. I thought that would have been self-explanatory. Your soul, John's soul and, to my surprise, *Bill's* soul will no longer roam free. I consent that my loyal assistant," she gestured to show them who she was referring to, before she continued, "will take you all."

Damian had reappeared in human form and was standing near John and Susan. "You need to stop this ludicrous behaviour immediately," he tried to assert. He fumbled about in his trouser pocket and retrieved a thin silver chain with a crucifix attached. He held it out in front of him, dangling from his fingertips.

"What do you think I am? A vampire?" Lisa mocked. *What a peculiar little character he is. Why the hell is he pretending to be a priest? Whatever will he be next?* She reached forward and grabbed the trinket from Damian's hand and threw it into the tree. *He's courageous, yet always very foolish.* "It's hard to believe that we actually originate from the same species, but why do always insist on pretending to be an angel?"

Damian did not try to stop Lisa. He couldn't because he knew his place.

A muffled thud stopped their half-hearted standoff. It was Derek's head that had fallen away from the tree trunk and onto the ground. It rolled several inches before it was stopped by one of the large root humps. They watched as smoke blew out of every orifice and then his head crumbled, along with Linda's body. Both turned to ash and got carried along in the breeze.

"This is the work of the devil," Damian called out. "We must destroy that tree before it's too late." He reached to pick up the bloodstained axe, but he was too slow as it was already in the black shadow's grasp. The axe flew into the air, over the trees and landed in the river.

Lisa ran a fingernail along the grooves of the pentangle as she pressed her body against the tree. "And you would know all about that, wouldn't you? What with you being a demon yourself. You only want this portal destroying so that you can try to get full reign without any conflict, but not in this lifetime or the next. You will always be the runt of the litter."

There was no response.

Lisa turned around. Everyone was gone. There was only her 'Curator Angelus' and the quintuplets for company.

Chapter Seventeen
The Burial

Lisa gave two quick bursts on her car horn as she waited outside the gates of Elizabeth's home. She tapped her fingers on the steering wheel as she looked around for signs of life. The gates began to open. There was no one there to greet her as she drove up the drive. She looked into her rear-view mirror and noted that the gates were closing behind her. It felt eerie, as she had expected, but something else was wrong. The atmosphere was heavy.

Susan's car was parked in the same place, but there was another car parked next to it. There was no one inside. It was long, black and looked official. Lisa did not recognise it. She parked next to it, switched off the engine and reached across to the passenger seat for her bag. Climbing out of her car, she slammed the door behind her and listened as the sound echoed against the silence. She aimed the key fob at the car and pressed it. The car beeped and flashed its lights.

Lisa could feel that someone was watching her. She turned around and looked up and saw that Peter was waving at her from one of the bedroom windows. His nose was pressed against the pane, but he was gone before she had chance to wave back.

As Lisa approached the door, it opened, and a smartly dressed gentleman appeared. Elizabeth was standing behind him. Her eyes looked puffy and sore. The gentleman turned to shake her hand.

"Thank you so much for all your help," Elizabeth said. She looked worn out as she had not been able to sleep the night before.

"If there's anything else you need, then please don't hesitate to contact either me or the office. There's usually always someone there manning the phone. The number is on the back of my card. Now, you take care, Mrs Caplin."

Standing to one side, Lisa allowed the gentleman to pass her. He gave her a polite smile and nodded as he walked by. She watched as he got into the black car and began to reverse out. The gates were opening as he turned his car around on the drive. He waited for a moment longer before he continued on his way. The gates began to close behind him.

Elizabeth walked back inside the house. She did not speak to Lisa, but left the door open for her to follow.

"I got here as soon as I could, Mum. Who was that?" Lisa realised that she sounded more jovial than what she should have done. She stood on the doormat and took off her trainers. There was a hole in her left sock where the nail of her big toe had gone through. Her feet were swollen after her drive. She started to rub them.

Peter slid down the staircase on his belly, feet first. His pyjama bottoms had risen and twisted. He got to the bottom stair, turned around, sat and waved at Lisa. She smiled back at him.

"It was the undertaker," Elizabeth said.

Lisa looked around the room. "Where's Robert?"

"He's still away on business."

"Does he know about Susan? Is he coming back to be with you?"

"Of course he knows about Susan. Don't you think I talk to my husband?" Elizabeth snapped before she burst into tears.

Lisa led Elizabeth to the sofa and helped her to sit. She had noticed the alcohol on her breath and her body odour. It was hard not to. Susan's death was one reason for Elizabeth's drinking, but her loneliness was another element to her alcohol dependency.

"He'll be back as soon as he can. He's a very busy man," Elizabeth said. She snivelled into her hands.

Peter got to his feet. He looked sad. He did not like to see his grandmother upset.

Lisa looked around the room. "Have they taken Susan's body away?" She realised that it was a stupid question, but the words had already passed her lips and could not be taken back. *No, she's having a bloody lay down on the sofa, Lisa!*

"Yes, she's at the mortuary."

"Would you like me to help you with the funeral arrangements?"

"No, there's no need. Karl's going to come up and help to sort things out."

"That's good."

There was an uncomfortable silence which only lasted a couple of minutes but felt more like hours.

"I know that my timing's a little bit off, but would it be okay if Peter and I stayed here for a while? It's just that the hotel is costing me a fortune. I wasn't expecting to be still living there and we could keep you company while Robert's away. You did offer before. Do you remember? I've been given the heads-up about a house coming onto the market very soon, so we shouldn't be under your feet for too long."

"Yes," Elizabeth answered, but all she could think about was that final image of Susan. *I just wish that I hadn't taken so long to choose that bottle of wine. I might have been able to save her. I will start going to those AA meetings and get some help.* She had never given it a second thought as to why the cellar door got stuck once and only on that particular day.

Looking at Peter, Lisa held out her arms. He ran towards her. The sound of his bare feet thumped against the floor. It was usual for Elizabeth to turn and tell him to walk, but she didn't. Lisa picked him up. They hugged and watched as Elizabeth got up from the sofa and made her way towards the window. She stared down at the lake.

Lisa saw the friction burn on the back of Peter's neck, but she said nothing. She did not need to ask, how or who, because she already knew the answer. "Do you want to help get our luggage from out of the boot, Peter?" she asked, "I'm sure that there will be enough room in your bedroom for me as well, won't there?"

Elizabeth turned her head to look at Lisa and Peter. Her expression was blank. It was obvious to everyone around that she was a broken woman. She was lost and unsure what to do or where to turn next.

What are you thinking when you look at us, Mum? Do you wish that it was Susan standing here instead of me? Do you wish that it was me that drowned in the lake?

"Yes, go on then," Peter said after he had pretended to mull over Lisa's questions.

The day of Susan's funeral arrived. It was an overcast day with the occasional spits of rain. Karl had made arrangements for her to be buried in a graveyard in the grounds of an old chapel that was close to Elizabeth's house. Karl's feelings were in tatters, but he was still considerate to Elizabeth's needs. He had known about the affair and that it had been going on for a number of years. If he felt any resentment, he did not show it.

Karl sat beside Robert and Elizabeth on the front pew. Karl and Susan's two daughters were not present. Nobody, except Karl, knew the reasons why and no one asked.

Grandma and Granddad Buckley were sitting on the pew behind them. They had flown over from Spain the night before. They were staring at the closed coffin.

Grandma and Granddad Parkins were stuck in traffic somewhere on the M6 or so they had claimed.

Lisa arrived at the funeral and parked her car, close to the chapel, on one of the side roads. She was sure that she recognised Mel and Damian as they walked away from the chapel in the opposite direction. She walked along the path, under the wooden archway and through the graveyard towards the chapel's entrance. There were a number of headstones that had subsided alongside the new ones, but it looked like someone took good care of the place. She looked over at a hole in the ground that had a large mound of soil to the side of it. *That'll probably be Susan's final resting place.*

Lisa walked into the chapel and down the aisle to the front. She reached the front pew, but when Elizabeth looked at her, she shuffled herself and her bag along so that there was not enough room for her to sit next to her.

What's got into her? Lisa stood there and waited for some sort of an explanation. *She was fine this morning. We were talking over breakfast. What's happened since then?* But Elizabeth continued to ignore her and stared with a blank expression at the coffin. Grandma and Granddad were doing the same.

Making her way to the back of the chapel, Lisa felt out of place as she sat down on the pew, alone.

Lisa began looking around and marvelled at the chapel's architecture and the stained-glass window at the front. There was a mustiness that filled the air, but didn't all old buildings smell like that?

For a moment, Lisa found herself back at Elizabeth's house. She was hovering in one of the corners of the kitchen ceiling and looking down at Peter who was playing with his toy cars on the floor. Eliza stormed in and started to shout at him. She reached down to grab his...

Lisa woke to the vicar finishing the service with a prayer. He walked down the aisle to the doors at the back of the chapel. Everyone began following him out into the graveyard. It had started to rain. They congregated around where Susan's coffin would be lowered into the ground and waited. Nobody spoke. Lisa stared into the hole. *I've got to make my excuses. I need to get out of here. Peter's in danger!*

Lisa looked at Elizabeth who was struggling to stand as she swayed from side to side. *She's intoxicated. She can't even stay sober for her own daughter's funeral.* Karl and Robert were holding her up.

The pallbearers, who were carrying Susan's coffin, arrived. They were six young men who volunteered in their spare time.

A black shadow and five smaller ones came into view behind the vicar. Lisa appeared to be the only one that could see them.

Shit! Is that why Eliza kept going on about Peter being too young to be going to a funeral and she suggested that she should look after him. Her eyes widened and she gulped out loud. *Who the hell is this Eliza? I don't know anything about her.*

So that the others would not notice her panic, Lisa appeared to be calm as she started to walk away from the graveside. She doubted that anyone would miss her anyway. When she reached the path, she picked up her pace until she ran out under the archway and made her way back to the car. The black shadows followed.